Murder at Sea

Murder at Sea

A

Mystery

WALTER STEWART

Published by Falken Arts
Los Angeles, California
First publication printing 2022

CHAPTER 1

It was a terrific summer day in Los Angeles. The sun was shining, the people were happily out and about, and the city had shaken off the dreary cold of the winter and the wet spring that had followed with a voluptuous abandon of flowers and blooming plants of every kind that festooned the metropolis like a lavish festival.

That's a lie.

It was a horribly hot Saturday plunk in the middle of Hollywood—over ninety-nine degrees to be exact. A crowd mostly of oldsters stood soaked in their own sweat around a hole in the ground at Hollywood's celebrated midtown cemetery for a final goodbye to a trusted and valued friend who had been involuntarily trundled off to the next world for his final reward.

Jerry Hearst had croaked—the guy who was the expert on the down and dirty of old Hollywood. The guy who Barney knew from like way back. The guy who'd helped Taylor on the Praetorius case, the Foster case, and a couple of others. At over 109 years of age, he finally died peacefully in his sleep and metaphorically with his boots on. Jerry was quite a character—quite a character. A good man. And... he was gone.

As Taylor stood next to Barney at the edge of the pile of friends and people who seemed to come out of nowhere, he couldn't help remembering the first time he met Jerry and listened to the tales he told of life in old Hollywood— particularly in the twenties through forties—when he used to hang out with the likes of Tom Mix, Ken Maynard, Hoot Gibson, Tim McCoy, Yakima Canutt, Buck Jones, William S. Hart, a young John Wayne, and a bunch of other guys. Most of those fellas were hard-livin' and hard-drinkin' regular guys who were more at home riding their horses in the dust, dirt, and sagebrush than driving their Pierce Arrows, Duesenbergs, Bugattis, and Auburns on the paved streets of La La Land. Most of these guys also disappeared from the public eye when interest in Westerns faded—except for a couple of them who understood that they had to re- invent themselves. Thus, the great John Wayne carved out a long career for himself playing all kinds of different parts. Tim McCoy got himself an afternoon TV show. And Bob Steele traded in his spurs and took on the seminal role as the vicious and sadistic Lash Canino in Bogart's *The Big Sleep.*

And now another bit of that history was going into the cold, cold ground to be lost and almost forgotten except for the celluloid vestiges that remained to tell the tale and, of course, the mourners who stood by him now.

"Jesus, what a loss," muttered Barney who was standing next to Taylor. "I can't believe it," he said with that tone of disbelief people always express when facing the reality that a friend, loved one, or associate has moved on since no one ever believes they will actually die and are shaken when someone close to them does. But it doesn't do any good to try to oppose death. Death's always the winner.

Taylor was just going to respond with something sage of his own when someone tapped his right arm. He turned to see a grim blue patrolman standing there in his black jackboots, trim outfit that bristled with a mic, gun, nightstick, and reflective aviator shades like the ones Mort Mills wore— the cop who questions Janet Leigh on the highway in *Psycho.* The reflective shades were meant to intimidate, but nothing and no one ever intimidated Taylor.

"Lieutenant Mott wants to see you," the man stated leaving out the word "now" that was nevertheless implied and certainly understood.

Taylor exhaled wearily. "See you later. Got a hot date," he cracked to Barney who turned with a frown on his face as Taylor followed the cop.

Another cop drove Taylor in a squad car to their destination without exchanging a single word between them. What would have been the use anyway. The cop knew the way, and Taylor didn't have anything he wished to share with this guy anyway.

They drove down Santa Monica to La Brea and then turned north to Sunset. The cop made a left and drove straight out towards the posh part of town and eventually into the chichi precincts of the Beverly Hills Hotel. He headed directly to the black and white portico with the broad red carpet and stopped.

"He's in bungalow five," he said and waited for his passenger to get out. Taylor sagged a little inside with a presentiment of what awaited him before he opened the door.

He exited the squad car and sighed hoping against hope that what he suspected he'd find, he wouldn't. But that was a childish wish. If Mott was there, he knew he'd been called because it was as bad as it gets. Stuff associated with Mott was *always* bad news.

He walked through the hotel entrance, through the lobby, and out of the main building to where the bungalows were located. He knew the hotel layout like the back of his hand, having been to the place about a gazillion times—or so it seemed. In a second he walked up the Spanish-tiled stairway and to the Spanish-styled bungalow Number 5.

The place was cordoned off with yellow police tape, and a blue cop stood at the door asking who he was. After identifying himself, he was let into the room.

It was milling with people taking prints and pictures, all of them wearing powder-blue covers over their shoes as though they were attending a baby shower. Taylor was told not to touch anything and was given a pair to slip on so as not to obliterate trace evidence. Then he walked over to Lieutenant Theodosius Mott who stood fat and sassy in his pork-pie hat. When he saw Taylor, he wiggled his finger for him to join him.

"Strange place for a cop convention," quipped Taylor as he joined Mott.

"Murders are always inconvenient and always invite an assemblage of official people like... well, like me."

"Murder?" Taylor shot back.

"Yep," replied Mott shortly as he turned to his right and stepped back a little. "This nice young lady," he indicated with sweep of the arm and an open palm, "is now the prima donna in a homicide."

The lady was semi obscured from view and lying on her back wedged against the rear of an antique-green couch. A man who was bending over her stood up with a thermometer in his rubber-gloved hand.

"Looks like she's cooled about twenty-five percent, and rigo's already set in. That makes it about twelve hours or so... about 2 a.m.," stated the man as he chewed his gum. Then he smiled broadly.

"Hey, squad leader. What the hell are you doing here?" asked Taylor's old compadre, Malcolm.

"Beats me. They wanted to see me, so here I am."

"Well, it's not as simple as all that," cut in Mott. "There's always a legitimate reason. We aren't the Gestapo."

Taylor stifled a laugh. "Really? You and the FBI coulda fooled me," he cracked. "So why am I here?" he pressed.

Mott suddenly produced a card between the middle and forefinger of his rubber-gloved hand like a cheap magician. "This yours?" he asked.

"Yeah, of course. You know it is," replied Taylor without even looking at the business card of Pierce

Investigations. "I was paid to guard her. So what?" he replied.

"Not very successfully, it seems," returned Mott with a smirk.

"That'd be pretty funny if she weren't dead," riposted Taylor.

"Sorry. I didn't mean that," apologized Mott.

"Forget it. Anyway, I got let off the gig," Taylor explained.

"When?"

"Last night."

"Well, we have to check out everything, even if it involves guys we've known a while."

"Um," grunted Taylor.

"So, when'd you see her last—precisely?" queried Mott.

Taylor searched his memory. "Um, precisely? Had to be about nine thirty last night. Like I said, she took me off the payroll. Said she didn't need me anymore. Said she already sent Harry a check. I said okay, left the premises, went home, and hit the sack an hour after Perry Mason was on at eleven thirty."

"Which episode?"

"'The Case of the Twice Told Twist,'" responded Taylor without losing a beat. "The only old Perry show of the sixties that was filmed in full color."

"You with anyone, or did anyone see you?" Mott prodded.

"Not a soul. Not even Abby," replied Taylor. "Watched the show and the news alone then cashed out for the day."

"Hey, Lieutenant," put in Malcolm suddenly. "I was in the corps with this guy for five, freakin', gut-wrenching years through thick and thin. You can believe anything he says."

Mott smiled. "And I've known him for, what, a dozen years or so?"

"Something like that," returned Taylor. "Anyway, how'd she die," he asked.

"See for yourself, squad leader," said Malcolm as he stepped back and invited Taylor to view the corpse.

"Oh, Christ!" exclaimed Taylor as he got a full view of what used to be Mrs. Brooke Cameron, formerly of Asheville and Durham, North Carolina and more recently of Brentwood California who now resembled nothing so much as a bloody pile of raw hamburger.

From what he could make out, she'd been gutted from low on her belly almost up to her neck and hacked up after that. It looked at first blush like Jack-the-Ripper with an attitude denoted by the additional lacerations that made the kill easily as hideous as those that that maniac committed. In fact, the amount of gore was so incredible that it would have made an unpracticed person puke their guts out. But Taylor had seen injuries as bad as this and, incredibly, even worse during his travels in the corps—just not in Beverly Hills.

"She'd been threatened by her ex," he volunteered as he stared blankly at the bloody remains. "She was only twenty-five and hired us herself to look after her. Her husband's this stockbroker, Anson Cameron. Rich but extremely, and I mean *stupidly* jealous. Thought she was stepping out on him at least from what she told us. I checked and she wasn't, but she had an impossible time trying to convince him. He roughed her up a few times. In fact, it finally got so bad that she had to get away from their home in Brentwood. We suggested here, and she moved in two weeks ago. I checked her every day and Harry and I were on call 24/7 if she needed anything. Then last night, big surprise! She said she'd straightened things out and didn't need us anymore. I was skeptical, but she shook my hand, said thanks, and that was pretty much that."

Mott took off his hat and sat back on the arm of a wingback chair. "We already have the husband..."

"Of course," interjected Taylor.

"Yeah, of course. But he maintains he didn't do it and has witnesses."

Taylor nodded the nod of one who'd heard the same thing umpteen times from umpteen perps. "Well, that's pretty much your problem, Lieutenant," he replied. "Meanwhile, I'm gonna take off. You know where to reach me if you need me," he added.

"Yeah, yeah, right. Okay," replied Mott as he stared dumbly at the grotesque mess on the floor.

"You can catch me too at the office. I'll let you know what we turn up after the autopsy," put in Malcolm as he followed Taylor out of the room.

Once outside on the patio, Taylor stopped to take in a great breath.

"As much as I've seen of that stuff, you still never get used to it," he said as Malcolm walked up.

"Just part of the job for me," responded his compadre. "Only the faces change. The rest is pretty much the same stuff. It's kind of funny," he observed as he gazed out over the hotel's enclosure. "People these days are always droning on in highfalutin' terms about race, diversity, and equity, but believe me, once they die, they're all just pretty much inert, dead tissue." He waited for some kind of sage response from

Taylor, but there wasn't one. "Anyway, you goin' back to your office?" he asked.

"Yeah, have to get an Uber ride back," replied Taylor.

"Naw, I'll take you," he volunteered. "My limos parked in the lot behind the bungalows."

"I didn't know there was a lot back there."

"That's because you haven't gotten as many 3 a.m. calls in the morning over the years as I have—for here and for the Chateau Marmont."

It turned out that Malcolm's "limo" was one of the county's older meat wagons—a noisy, bouncy ride that needed new struts and a repair to the exhaust or the catalytic converter since fumes were leaking into the passenger compartment. Taylor also winced at the lingering frowsy odor from the departed whom they routinely transported in the back; but he soon became accustomed to all of it and quite nose blind. The pair talked over some of the old days and the guys with whom they shared their experiences, finally deciding it was high time that they all had a get-together—the ones who were still around and in town... and those who were still vertical, at any rate.

Malcolm dropped Taylor off at the office and then drove away in a cloud of exhaust smoke. Since Barney had driven the two of them to Jerry's funeral, his own car was still just where he left it.

"Yer late," came the ever-cheerful greeting from the office's ever-cheerful distaff majordomo with the red hair and redder lips as he walked through the door.

"It was a funeral. Then a murder," he stated.

"My, my, you *do* get around," quipped Marge. "I'd say you better get your tight little buns in Harry's office before he chews you a whole new one," she pronounced.

Taylor was too wiped out from the heat and dread of the day to shoot her a snappy comeback, so he turned and lumbered into Harry's office where he dropped himself into the oak chair in front of Harry's desk before the man could speak.

"Geez! It's mid-afternoon. Where the hell you been?" asked the gruff one as he stuck his cold cigar butt in his mouth and crooked his thumbs behind his suspenders in front.

"Hey, it's been a long day. First, I didn't even get to tell you that last night the Cameron dame dropped the case..."

"Aw, no!" whined Harry.

"Yeah, but she said she'd already sent you a check. Anyway, while I'm at the funeral for Jerry Hearst this afternoon, Mott called me to her bungalow because she'd been offed."

"Offed? What!" exclaimed Harry. "How?" he asked.

"Ya don't wanna know," replied Taylor. "It looked like a rage murder to me. Anyway, they suspect the husband naturally..."

"Naturally."

"And that's pretty much the end of that case on our end," stated Taylor with finality.

Harry slumped back into his chair in a long, uncharacteristic silence.

Taylor waited a second and then perked up. He was expecting one of Harry's usual tongue-lashings, but there was nothing but dead air. Taylor squinted at him. Then groaned.

"Okay, okay. So tell me now. Just what have you gone and volunteered me for?"

Harry winced. "Me?" he replied innocently. "Why would I volunteer you for something?"

"I don't know why, but you always do it, and I know it's somethin'. You ain't sayin', but it's somethin'; I can *always* tell."

"Gee, y'know, you haven't had a real vacation for a long time," remarked the scion of the establishment out of nowhere without losing a beat.

"Oh, Christ. Here it comes," responded Taylor with an even deeper groan as he wiped his hand across his mouth.

"Naw, I mean it," put in Harry, eager to vindicate himself. "I really mean it," he repeated, laying it on pretty thick.

Taylor sighed wearily. "Look, just cut to the chase. Just tell me what you've got me lined up for *this* time."

"You like families, don't you? Kids?"

Taylor regarded him skeptically. "No, not really. All kids do is eat, poop, and make trouble," he replied. "Just like the parents."

Harry pushed himself forward, elbows on his desk. "Look, this could be worth an absolute shitload of money for us."

"Then why don't you do it? Whatever it is?"

"I would, but it calls for a younger man. It's a week or so of bodyguarding a family on vacation. And the guy's not a phony-baloney; he'll pay up front."

Taylor looked up dully. "A trip for a week, with a family," he echoed in a business-like tone. "They all going to stick together?"

"Absolutely. But it's really only the father of the fam that needs looking after. And the kids will have a nanny."

"A nanny. Hm, that's not bad," Taylor responded somewhat heartened. "So, *what about* the guy?"

"He's *the* accountant for Randall/Waring Inc.—that big brokerage house and a bunch of other firms I can't even name. Seems the government is doing an audit of these companies, and he's the expert they want to focus on."

"What? He embezzled, stole, or otherwise mucked with the company funds?"

"On the contrary, this guy's cleaner than Lady Liberty's long underwear, but you know how the government works."

"Or mostly doesn't work... the corrupt bastards," Taylor cracked. "So what's the beef?"

"The beef is, apparently there are guys out there who may not want him to speak to the government about what's been going on with their assets..."

"And surprise, surprise... the government won't protect him..."

"Which is why he wants us. And the best part for me is that this guy's not one of those splashy celebs who'll demand everything then skip on the bill. Not this guy," concluded Harry.

Taylor folded his lip as he considered the parameters of the case and what he'd have to do to protect the man even if a nanny was there to watch the whelps. Finally, he nodded his head. "If that's all it is, then yeah, I think I can cover it."

"Then you're saying *you will take the case?*" said Harry with a peculiar emphasis on Taylor's agreement.

Taylor looked askance at him. "Yeah, I said it. I agree to take the case. I said it already. Geesch!"

"Okay, then I'll have Marge do the usual background checks on everyone and scope the trip from start to finish."

Harry relaxed back into his chair and let out a breath. "That's great," he said. "Uh... there's only one little hitch to it—I mean, if you can even really call it a hitch?" he put in with a little, tentative chuckle.

Taylor smiled back quizzically. "Oh, yeah?" he returned innocently. "And what would that be?" he asked.

"Uh... you have to do this while the whole family is, uh... on a cruise. On a ship... On the water."

When it came right down to it, there were only two things that Taylor really couldn't abide: April 15th and bodies of water. He disliked April 15th not because it was the IRS's special day of government theft but rather because one of his closest friends dropped dead on that day. The other reason was what that lawyer at Lambert Group Banking, Chris Miller, had admitted to him a while back during the Dawn Fearing case, and it still echoed in his ears. It wasn't just the water: "The problem is sharks. You can't trust sharks," Miller stated. "You can never tell what they're up to. But whatever it is, it's always deadly."

Taylor didn't comment on what the guy said back then, and Miller had no way of knowing, but Taylor felt exactly the same for a couple of reasons. Like they claimed in vampire lore of old, Taylor also simply had a strong aversion to flying or traveling over water—just not for the same reason. And, as far as he was concerned, you also didn't have to be a pansy to have that point of view. One reason was that as a little kid, some friends took him to Catalina on a sailboat. They told him to climb the mast, and he did so obediently. Big laughs and chuckles all around. But it was only when he was near the top that he realized that the bobbing of the boat made the mast lean to one side over the water and then to the other side with the same point of view. Meanwhile, the hilarious drunken friends of the boat owner were shooting at sharks with 45s. Blood was all over the water, and as Taylor looked down, he could just imagine falling into the water right into the middle of that school of huge sharks circling the boat that were currently tearing their wounded brethren into shreds that made the water around the boat bright red with the flourishing gore of bloody death. It scared the hell out of the kid.

The other reason is that when he was in the corps, he met an old guy who had been on the Indianapolis—that ship that Robert Shaw told the tale of in *Jaws*. When Taylor jocularly asked if the situation was *really* as dire as painted in the movie, the guy just gave him a look without saying anything; but in that single look was *everything*. It needed no explanation or elaboration. Unfortunately, he had now given his word to Harry that he'd take the case, and over and across the waters he would go. After all, you never go back on your word.

People always asked why Pierce Investigations didn't take a lot of bodyguard jobs. After all, with the number of celebrities living in Hollywood and environs, they should have been relatively easy to find. The simple answer was that Harry got stung by a celebutard some years back and vowed he'd never take on a job like that again. Back then, he did the job, suffered all their ridiculous demands, and then they stiffed him on the payment. It ended up a three-year court case, and because the tard had a good lawyer, Harry won but only got expenses and court fees; that is, he broke even which is not a way to make a living in this business even if some people do.

Fact is, if you're positioned right and have a half-way honest client, you can actually pull down millions a year in Hollywood; that is, depending on the popularity of the client or his or her ego concerning their self-worth. In fact, things were better today for bodyguards than they were even twenty years ago. These days all of the bodyguards in La La Land have formed a kind of loose confraternity made of ex-military guys, retired wrestlers, boxers, and bouncers. Some dress in Brooks Brothers and bristle with all kinds of electronic paraphernalia, and some wear hoodies and let their sheer size do the talking. In fact, one guy who's employed by an A-lister is huge and looks like Sasquatch; nobody messes with this guy. The bottom line for these bodyguards is, everybody knows everybody else, who they work for, and about what they're paid—and no one tries to stiff anyone on a bill anymore. The only thing that's remained precisely the same are the celebutards' demands which are just as ridiculous today as they were back in the day. For instance, they absolutely must have things such as: bowls of single color M&Ms; fresh and specifically colored toilet seats; weird and specially-prepared meals and dishes; exotic, ultra-expensive alcohol brands; bizarre types of furniture—you name it. It's also principally because of such nonsense why Harry opted to avoid the ultra-famous for those who are not well-known but need protection anyway. Anyway, this time it meant a boat trip.

In order to get to the boat on which Taylor and the family were to embark on the trip, Taylor first had to fly to Florida to set up a cover. There he'd be picked up and then everyone would fly to Barcelona where the ship was docked. Yes, that meant, they had to fly over water, but the thought of that was cushioned somewhat by the fact that the whole thing was arranged to be top of the line. The Airbus was first class, roomy, and comfortable, and that made the trip over the Atlantic that much more bearable. Besides, Taylor didn't really mind a plane flight, just the water under it. After all, he'd jumped from planes a ton of times into inhospitable jungles and onto burning, desert locales when he was in the corps on secret jobs for "the man." But this time? Piece o' cake!

His first meeting with the family at the Florida stopover was rather perfunctory, but it turned out that they were actually less trouble than he'd anticipated. The two kids were a girl eight and a boy six. They were surprisingly well-mannered and taken care of by a nanny named Amanda Bannon. She was a quiet twenty-something dark brunette with big brown eyes and a nice smile who preferred to be called Mandy. She wore a white, short-sleeve shirt, knee-length shorts, and wore her hair in a ponytail which made her look very girlish. An altogether sweet girl, Taylor remarked to himself. She dealt with the children like a doting mother hen and guided them gently but surely with the confidence of someone who knew precisely what they were doing.

The daughter was Amy who was inquisitive and asked about everything. The boy was Curtis who sort of took a shine to Taylor and had all sorts of questions about what he did which, of course, he had to fabricate since he was under cover.

The mother, Cassandra or Cass to her husband, was a pretty-enough lady who was fully occupied with herself like one of those vapid reality-show dames—the kind of woman who never should have had kids in the first place because she didn't care about them as much as she cared about herself, her clothes, her weight and figure, her jewelry, her car, and a host of other non-essentials in life.

Lastly, the father and object of the whole exercise, Allen Wells, was quiet and didn't make a show of the fact that he had enough money to easily pay for what was going to be a half-million-dollar excursion by the time the whole thing was over. He was a little older, starting to go bald, and had a dad bod. Taylor found him likable because he, among all the big shots he ever met, was actually a regular no-BS guy who didn't put up with all the phony crap that usually attends wealth. He grew up in L.A. and went from LACC to UCLA where he earned an MBA and became a CPA for folks in the movie biz because he was razor-sharp and good at his job. From there his reputation spread, and he became sought after by giant corporations across the nation. He was married in his mid-twenties while he was working his way up the ladder of success, but it didn't take and made him gun shy of women until he met Cassandra a dozen years later at a New Year's Eve party. They lived together until she finally dropped the hammer on him and demanded either he'd marry her or she'd split. Having gotten very comfortable with their arrangement and not eager to break in another filly at this stage in his life, Wells opted for the former choice—but with a well-thought-out prenup so that his trophy wife couldn't just skip out if things went south. She bought it, astutely perceiving that even a smaller taste of the enchilada was better than no enchilada at all. Anyway, from Taylor's position, he could clearly see that these two had both gotten precisely what they wanted when they signed the license; he got the sexy Barbie doll, and she got a comfortable and luxurious set up for the rest of her natural life. Since then, they had the two kids—the daughter by Lamaze, and the son as a result of the mother's penchant for doing her daily yoga routine naked in front of the TV. Apparently, the husband nailed her in the midst of a downward dog position, and the result nine-months later was little Curtis. Anyway, everything was hunky-dory, well, until this meshugas with the customers' assets and accounting books came up. Taylor also had to smile because Wells admitted self-deprecatingly that he actually had hired him to take care of the wife and kids—not himself. As for the guys that might try to harm him personally, Wells merely spat: "Ef 'em!"

As for the protection that Wells was paying for, Taylor left his own firearms at home because to legally transport them meant dealing with a pile of government forms he'd have to fill out with almost some kind of presidential approval—although he knew full well that the current weaselly president hated guns to begin with. It wasn't worth it. If he needed a gun, he still had contacts in every European country from the old days who could fill his order with one call. Besides, who needs guns to get a job done. He knew how to kill people quickly and relatively silently with his bare hands; anyway, in comparison, firearms were cumbersome, loud, and too often a nuisance.

Aside from that, Taylor went incognito as one of Wells' distant cousins with whom he spent summers at Camp Potawatomi in Illinois years ago when they were kids. For a disguise, he posed as a middle-school math teacher from Palm Beach where he flew first to meet them. To make the disguise complete, he dressed in shabby-chic—a pair of geeky-framed glasses with transition lenses, casual Penny's short-sleeve shirts, polos, light Dockers with a worn, woven leather belt, and slip-on deck shoes. The glasses let him scan crowds and people unobtrusively, particularly whenever they were outdoors.

The flight out of Florida was okay. Taylor and the fam sat in five of the twenty first-class comfortable cubicles. Taylor had been warned by a stewardess he knew a couple of years back never to drink the water, coffee, or tea on a plane—not even in first class. That's because they seldom cleaned the water tanks. Nonetheless, he risked a couple of lattes that didn't taste half bad. But since the day he'd gotten food poisoning from a fish dinner on a British flight, he didn't eat anything but nuts and a selection of cheeses that they offered him—even if it *was* first class and meant passing up what was supposedly class-A fare. The nuts and stuff would have to tide him over until they reached their destination. He couldn't afford to get sick or even get an upset stomach.

Otherwise, the flight was unremarkable. Taylor didn't speak with anyone but the stewardesses. The family all sat close together in cubicles just ahead of him and seemed to have things well in hand. Mandy Bannon stayed with the kids who watched Disney cartoons, Wells worked on his computer, and the wife slept with a black mask over her eyes and snored luxuriantly. In fact, since he got to the check-in at the airport, Taylor hadn't talked with anyone at all, well, besides a twenties-something guy named Bob Ross who took a seat beside him in the lounge before take-off. The guy, who was all youthful energy, struck up a more or less one-sided conversation with Taylor about fast cars, faster planes, and a new airborne bike powered by kerosene that could reach fifteen-thousand feet and had a twenty-minute range. He'd seen it go through its paces online. "Man, was that *sweet*," he kept saying. It was the kind of tech talk which Taylor didn't mind. Besides, Ross seemed affable enough. Said he was taking this flight to join his fiancée, Tabitha, who was visiting family in Germany. They'd planned this trip to the Mediterranean with the final destination of Athens for over a year. They'd even be taking the same ship as Taylor and the fam. Maybe they could take meals together.

Taylor waved to him as they boarded, and Ross headed for his seat in the main cabin while Taylor was up front. They also exchanged a friendly nod once more when Taylor spotted him in an aisle seat when he went to use one of the heads in the main cabin of the plane since the first class one had a line of people in front of it. He exchanged a few words with him until a stewardess tapped him on the shoulder and reminded him that he was first-class and should use the rest room there. Taylor replied that he didn't think there was any difference and wanted to chat with his friend anyway—just to make the officious stewardess' life as difficult as she deserved. "As you please," she said and then walked off.

Taylor bid good-bye to Ross and then made for the head. By the time he returned, it looked like the kid was sound asleep.

The rest of the flight was routine. He snacked on nuts, cheese, and other packaged fare, drank a couple of Cokes, and watched an Avenger movie and an idiotically rotten horror film about people getting old on a beach. Afterwards, he closed his eyes and slept until the plane's captain came over the PA system and announced that they were thirty minutes out from landing.

After that, people started gathering themselves and their stuff together including Wells, the wife, and Mandy and the kids. Taylor watched the landscape beneath him go by as the altitude of the plane decreased until it was roof-top high. Then there was the familiar "ert" sound of the tires as they touched down on the tarmac. The plane landed and then made it to the terminal where it finally came to rest with a little bounce like a car hitting a parking stop at the grocery store.

Instantly, people got up and started gathering their coats and carry-ons from the overheads. Taylor remained extra alert to anyone who even looked sideways at Wells and his brood, since the most dangerous time of a trip like this was always the transits from one place to another—in this case, until they reached their cabins on the ship. It took about five more minutes for the crush of people to begin to debark, and slowly the crowd emptied the plane.

When the main cabin of the plane was emptied, one of the stewardesses noticed that a passenger was still in his seat, probably asleep. But when she shook his shoulder, his head fell to the side. His eyes were open and drool ran from his mouth. Her first reaction was all she could do to keep from screaming, but that's where her training kicked in. She calmly but insistently waved to another stewardess to join her, and the two of them tried to rouse the man but to no avail. Youthful Bob Ross was dead. There was no doubt about it. Like Scrooge's Old Marley—he was dead—dead as a doornail.

CHAPTER 2

Taylor stood with the family group in the terminal and continued to keep an eagle eye on them and on anyone who looked suspicious from behind the shadowed lenses of his Ray Bans while they waited for their transportation. After being checked by customs, their luggage would be picked up by the cruise company with whom they had booked, and they would be taken directly to the ship in a limo, not with the busses that other passengers might take. After all, for Wells it was the most secure way for them to travel, and besides, Wells was paying top dollar for this excursion, and this was just another perk of one of those fancy-schmanzy trips on a huge ship that had all the amenities of an amusement park.

Taylor found it interesting that Wells hadn't set up the trip to take on one of those big, expensive private yachts—even though he certainly had the moolah to do so. After all, there would be fewer people and fewer headaches all around concerning his security. But when he asked him, Wells had a reasonable, indeed quite intelligent response.

"I've been on a number of private yachts like that," he explained, "but, you see, they're not all they're cracked up to be."

Taylor raised his eyebrows quizzically recalling his associations with the hoi polloi in Hollywood who spent money like water renting big yachts and planes so that they could fill up their wasted, idle hours doing whatever they wanted to do.

"Yachts!" spat Wells deprecatingly. "Yeah, I've done yachts—a bunch of times. Ya wanna know about yachts?" he asked and in a tone you wouldn't want to dismiss.

"Shoot!"

"Okay, let's say you book a charter on one of those big yachts for a week. If it's one of those ultra-yachts that cost over $120 million, chances are pretty good that it's been used by plenty of high rollers—principally sports figures and their friends and girlfriends. Jesus, what pigs! I mean, even if they've meticulously cleaned the cabins with Q-tips and antiseptics, it's near impossible to completely eradicate the smell of debauchery, pot, smoked cocaine, and vomit left behind by partygoers that sort of seeps into everything. Anyway, I can always smell it."

Taylor nodded understanding.

"And if you check the mattresses, nine times out of ten you'll find stains of every disgusting sort left by people who'd been there before. They just love to grease up with tanning oil or cover themselves in sunscreen and don't have the courtesy to wash off properly before they hop in the sack to do whatever else they wanna do in there. Or maybe they just ate fried chicken in bed and soiled it that way. Who wants to expose their kids to that! Either way, it's pretty disgusting. Add to that the fact that you may have to fork out more cash for extras they didn't tell you about when you signed up, and in the end you get to tip them for the poor service you received, and pretty heavily, even if things were done in a half-assed fashion," Wells complained.

"Sounds like you've had a lot of experience."

"You bet your sweet ass I have," he confirmed. "Not to say that all of the big ships and cruise lines are faultless, of course. I've been on several of those cruises where people got sick and spread a norovirus across the whole ship. Jesus, people puking in the hallways and all over the deck and..." Wells stopped himself. "All I'm saying is that you've got to be careful about which cruise you take," he added in a more measured tone. "That's why we're taking the *Flying Cloud*, British registry with an entire British crew. It's part of that entertainment company that makes movies, owns fun resort parks, and caters to kids. They've even got things like little race cars for the boys, and princess stuff for the girls."

"So that's why this one?" Taylor queried.

Wells lit up. "Yeah. I've taken this line three times, and it's been a wonderful experience every time. No detail is overlooked. No concern is too small to be rectified. The cruise folks are even taking our luggage to our suites at this very moment. Everything about the ship is professionally done. Add to that the fact that the ship's designed for families and kids and that they're well taken care of the entire time and have plenty to do. They even have water slides on this damn thing. And lastly, the cuisine is excellent. They've got anything you want. Mr. Taylor ..."

"Cousin Taylor," the other corrected.

"Right. Anyway, I dare say you'll be able to get the best latte you've ever had, and it'll be just as excellent every time you get it."

Taylor squinted a little. "Now them's pretty tall words, pardner," he responded with a hint of jocular skepticism in his voice.

Wells laughed. "Don't worry, you'll see. You'll see," he insisted. "Anyway, we'll be there soon enough. By the way," he added, interrupting himself, "you haven't seen anything to be concerned about yet, have you?" he questioned.

Taylor shook his head in the negative. "Don't worry, cousin. As I said when you brought me on, if I have the slightest concern about anything at all, I'll let you know right away if I don't kill the guys first."

"Just not in front of the kids," replied Wells with a little chuckle. "But I suppose we'd better get to the limo now."

"Be right there," responded Taylor. "I have to check in with the office and report on our progress," he said and stepped away from the group a few paces and took out his phone.

His first call was to Abby who wasn't at home. He left a message that all was well and yadda, yadda, yadda. He missed her and he'd call her tomorrow. Then he punched in the office number and waited. Marge answered with her usual acrid greeting. Yeah, she'd give Harry his report, she knew the drill, and did he think she was stupid or something? And yeah, even if he didn't care to ask, everything was okay in the office except that Bernstein brought his girlfriend, the mortuary girl, to the office, and she couldn't see what Bernstein saw in her. Her niece Nadine was ten times better than that shiksa—prettier and more accomplished. Anyway, Taylor ought to get his little cushy tushy back pronto instead of lollygagging around with the "swells" because the court papers were piling up. And oh yeah, he got a message from that cop, Lieutenant Mott, she reported with distain in her voice because she disliked cops. "And what was that?" he asked. "He said to tell you that the husband's been cleared. Had an air-tight alibi, whatever that means," she said.

He asked if she really said "swells," which elicited a hailstorm of criticism about how well she did her job and was never appreciated and never...

"Okay, o—kaaay," he returned exasperated as he shook his head. "just a little harmless joke," he added.

"A joke?!" came the whine over the line. "Why, I..."

"Okay, already. Jesus!" he exclaimed. "I'll check in tomorrow. Tell Bernstein to get you a doughnut," he put in which elicited the beginnings of yet another tirade although this time, instead of listening or answering back, he quickly said good-bye to which she replied, "Yeah, whatever," and hung up.

As he stuffed his phone back into his pocket, he pondered Mott's message to him. Brooke Cameron had been murdered, but not by the husband. Hm! Curious, he thought. And an air-tight alibi. On the other hand, he wondered why she shut down the case so precipitously. And if it was a rage killing, who else wanted her dead so bad as to mutilate her in that way? Or was the killing only made to look that way? Could be. After all, even after ex-coroner Thomas Noguchi stated that Marilyn Monroe's death was an accidental overdose, some still thought that it was murder—and they were anything but crackpots. Like Harry always said, it was well known that there were two guys who had it in for Marilyn big time and could easily have covered it up with all of the power of the government behind them—powerful, married men who took advantage of Marilyn and made lying promises to her just so that they could screw the Movie Queen on the side. And then they had somebody murder her in a way that wouldn't show and couldn't be spotted even by someone as competent as Thomas Noguchi. It was the kind of slight-of-hand at which an agency like the CIA was expert.

But no time to mull over an old job that was completely out of his hands; Mott would have to see to the final disposition of Brooke Cameron's case.

The black limo pulled up, and the fam piled in. As the last one to get in the car, Taylor scanned the area to ensure it was clear before he climbed aboard. He squeezed into the space next to Mandy with young Curtis on the facing seat.

"Are you goin' on the water slide with us, Cousin Taylor?" queried Curtis.

"Curtis!" cut in Mandy. "You know better than to bother Cousin Taylor," she chided.

Taylor chuckled. "No, it's all right," he responded to the eager youngster. "I'm not a big fan of water slides, Curtis. But I might just watch a couple of DVDs and catch some rays with you."

"Stream," shot back the youngster. "Nobody watches DVDs anymore. Everybody streams," spoketh the young know-it-all.

"Right. Streaming," returned Taylor, correcting his hideous technological *faux pas.* "You seem to know an awful lot about this tech stuff. You *are* just six, aren't you, Curtis?" he asked with a disarming smile.

"Six-and-a-half," he corrected, "but I watch shows all the time, so I know about that stuff—especially the Avengers against the bad guys."

"Well," responded Taylor with a chuckle, "I doubt that we'll run into any bad guys on this trip. Besides, I'm more at home with numbers than with movies."

Mandy smiled at Curtis. "Well," she said, "I doubt that we'll run into any real bad guys here—no evil Thanos, or Loki, or Nebula, or Star-Lord..."

"Star-Lord's a good guy," retorted young Curtis with a furrowed brow.

"Curtis," chimed in the father, "Didn't we ask you not to bother Mandy or our cousin with a lot of silly questions?" he queried rhetorically.

"Yes, dad," replied the kid sheepishly.

Mandy, laughed. "Don't worry, Curtis," she said. "You'll have plenty to do once we get to the ship and see all your galactic friends."

Taylor looked at her quizzically.

"Oh, didn't your cousin tell you?" she asked.

"Apparently not," he returned.

"Well, this isn't *just* a cruise, it's a fantasy cruise with all the characters from those Avenger and animated films. Great stuff for kids," she added with a happy chuckle.

"Terrific. I can hardly wait," replied Taylor, who hid his concerns about how such broad exposure on a boat full of kids and parents would affect his job.

"Al, how long is it going to take us to get to the ship?" asked Mrs. Wells out of nowhere with an irritated tinge to her voice.

"I don't know," he answered and beeped the chauffeur on the intercom.

"Alfonse, how long before we get to the ship?" he asked.

"Half-an-hour if there's light traffic," replied Alfonse.

"Why didn't you order the copter like I asked?" put in the missus in an exasperated tone.

"Tried," replied Wells. "They wouldn't do that here."

Mrs. Wells let out something like a sigh and a groan at the same time. "Well, another crappy start to another crappy vacation," she complained.

"Honey, the children," Wells chided.

"Oh, Allen, grow up," she charged. "They're going to learn all this language one day anyway if they already haven't gotten it off those movies they watch," she said.

"Yeah, dad. At least she didn't say it would be a 'shitty vacation,'" chimed in little Curtis to a bug-eyed response of the adults.

In fact, the ride took a little less time than expected during which the kids played a card game, the mother slept, and Wells held a conversation with Mandy Bannon about what the kids would be doing once on board. Taylor took the opportunity to get a little shuteye as the other two mapped out each day's activities in accordance with a printed guide that the cruise line made available. Then suddenly, they were at the ship.

Taylor woke with a start the second he sensed that the limo had stopped. Alfonse exited the driver's seat and opened the doors for the passengers. Since the luggage had already been forwarded to the ship, it was just a matter of gathering the few personal items that the passengers had brought with them. Wells handed Alfonse a hefty tip, and everyone headed for the reception desk and then for the gangplank.

Taylor kept a nonchalant close eye on the area and everything that went on, but nothing seemed to be out place, and the travelers passed onto the ship via the VIP ramp. Once on the ship, they took the lift up to the fourteenth deck on which their high-security suites were located.

Wells had reserved three staterooms for the whole group, although the term "stateroom" hardly covered it. Wells and his wife were in one two-bedroom stateroom as were Mandy Bannon and the kids. Taylor was in a one-bedroom all by himself. All three suites adjoined each other by individual verandas. And as the old saw went, the whole set up really was POSH—port out, starboard home, except that they were situated on the starboard side of the ship as it travelled east.

The staterooms were something to see. All the cabinets were tiger maple. The bathrooms had granite counters with cute little boxes of Elemis soap, richly tiled showers with a variety of shampoos, jacuzzi baths, TVs and other electronics galore—in short, everything and more than you'd expect in a top-end hotel room back home. The three stateroom suites that they had reserved were named the Imperial, the Royal, and the Majestic.

Mr. and Mrs. Wells had separate bedrooms because she was a light sleeper and he liked to stay up until three or four in the morning. Mandy and the kids also had a two bedroom stateroom with separate bathrooms so that she could more easily take care of and entertain them and still have some privacy. Lastly, Taylor's cabin was at the opposite end from them but was perfectly situated as a buffer against another family that was on his right flank and also had an individual veranda. In fact, every stateroom of the top two decks had its own veranda.

After Taylor squared away his stuff, he went to Wells' door and knocked softly. After a few seconds, the door opened and the man himself answered. Taylor spoke to him *sotto voce.*

"I'm going to scope out the ship and get something to drink. Think you'll be all right?" he asked.

"No problem," replied Wells. "Mind if I tag along?" he asked.

"And your wife?"

"Aah, she's out for her afternoon nap for a couple of hours."

Taylor nodded. "Then yeah, sure. Come along," he agreed.

"Just let me get my shoes on, and I'll be right with ya," he replied.

Wells left the door ajar and disappeared but in a second was back. He stepped out and shut the door and regarded the key and entrance pad next to the door. "In your experience, is this thing really any good for keeping people out?" he asked.

"Well, when we registered they took all that time checking our voices, accents, fingerprints, handprints, irises, retinas, facial movement, and matched everything to our DNA, and you'd think that'd be enough."

"Isn't it?" asked Wells.

"Maybe. But since I don't trust anyone, and especially not computers with which I've had some gnarly experience,

I'd say maybe... but for me all that's stuff's no great guarantee."

"So what do you suggest?" Wells asked.

"Here," said Taylor as he pulled a stray thread from his cheap shirt, licked it, and pasted it low between the door and the door jamb. "Now you'll know if anyone enters while we're gone."

Wells laughed like hell. "Old school. Man, I love that old-style, *Maltese Falcon* detective stuff," he declared brightly as the two headed off down the hallway.

"Really?" remarked Taylor.

"You bet," put in Wells. "I always wanted to be a detective, ya know. Before I hired you, I had you and some other guys checked out real good. You were the best. You never failed a client," he stated with not a little bit of admiration.

"It's not the easiest way to make a living," responded Taylor, "but it seems to present the world in which I function best," he added.

"Huh!" grunted Wells. "Could you tell me about it and give me some tips?" he asked.

"You got a couple of days for me to bend your ear?" Taylor shot back.

"For you?" he said. "You bet your sweet ass I do," he added, slapping Taylor on the back good-naturedly as the two continued down the hall to the elevator.

They made their way to the main deck where they ran a gauntlet of other passengers, old men and women, frazzled parents, and kids—lots of kids—tons of kids. They took some stairs to where some of the food venues were located, and there were a bunch of them. You could get chow like Italian and Mexican food at open buffets. Recalling that all the food and drinks—except for the alcoholic ones that were pre-paid, Taylor marveled at how the people jammed themselves around the buffets and gorged themselves on stuff that would add pounds and stomach problems later in the evening when sumptuous dinners would be served.

All the while, Wells continued to pump him for tricks of the trade and stories from the past about how he solved this or that case. In fact, Wells ran through a slew of his past cases in some detail as though he were rattling off the plot of some cheap pulp fiction detective yarns.

"You really *did* have me investigated," remarked Taylor.

"Sid told me."

"Berman?"

"Yeah, he's an old friend. I asked him for people who could protect me, and he gives me a list about a foot long.

Then I ask him for the best guy, and without the slightest hesitation he names you. Just you."

"I'm flattered," replied Taylor as they settled on the coffee bar where the barista brewed up any kind of coffee you could name and any way you wanted it.

"What can I get ya, mate," inquired the man behind the bar.

"A latte for me…"

"And straight espresso for me," put in Wells.

"Yes, sir," replied the fellow who had a cockney accent.

"I usually drink these to stay awake while I'm working," explained Allen. "Straight espresso plus a ton of sugar, like in that Brando flick, *The Freshman*, where he keeps pouring in spoonful after spoonful. There's nothing like it."

"Except maybe sleepless nights, tooth decay, and diabetes," returned Taylor.

Wells laughed like hell. "You're probably right—about the sleep, anyway. My doc says I'm in good shape. Hell, I pay him enough to keep me that way."

"Doctors?" replied Taylor. "I might trust 'em to take out a splinter—maybe even to remove a bullet. But with diseases, it's a different thing. I mean, I give it to 'em for tryin', but with diseases like diabetes, Alzheimer's, and MS, they're just guessing at how to deal with those. You ever seen anyone who had Ebola?"

"Naw."

"That's good. 'Cause you wouldn't want to. Once that sucker gets you, it's all she wrote."

"That lethal, huh?"

"And then some."

Wells was going to ask another question, but before he could, a slim, swarthy guy in an Armani shirt with a silk-embroidered crest on the pocket stepped up to the bar next to Taylor.

"Arabica," he ordered before the barista could speak. "With warm cream," he added in a crisp British with the added edge of an eastern accent.

"Yes, sir," replied the fellow dutifully as he went to work. In a second he handed the man his beverage.

"Thank you..."

"I'm Mike," replied the barista.

"Then thanks, Mike," the man said. He put the cup down and spooned in some sugar. Then he lifted the cup to his lips and drank soulfully.

"Looks good," Wells put in out of nowhere.

The man regarded him with a bright smile. "Not bad for ship's fare."

Taylor took a good look at the fellow. He was about five-ten, 160 pounds, and athletic from the way that he carried himself. Obviously from wealth as his finely manicured nails and sharply cut beard indicated. He was British educated from the tone of his voice but a native of the Mideast, probably an Egyptian, according to his looks. His smile was warm and ingratiating. He was either real nice or the kind of guy who would slit your throat while eating a fig. Or perhaps he was a loving father of nine kids who just needed a java break.

"Family having fun?" Taylor asked the man.

The fellow's eyebrows rose at the question. "Yes. My wife and daughter have gone to the movies," he replied.

"Which?" pressed Taylor. "Our little ones are at one of those Avenger movies. Tried to get us to go, but you know..." he put in offhandedly.

The fellow smiled affably and managed a little laugh. "Yes, yes," he replied. "Little boys seem to love all that action. The only thing they leave out is the gallons of blood that would be all over the place."

"Yes, terrible," responded Wells. "Such violent films."

"Which is why my daughter likes the princess films. No one gets injured, and no one gets hurt."

"Well, maybe just a bruised ego or two," put in Taylor to which all three laughed.

"For a guy, almost worse than getting killed sometimes," ventured Wells.

"Yes, unceremoniously dumped by a member of the opposite sex—the ultimate come down! And how many of *those* have I suffered," he added to which the others laughed along with him.

"Have we *all* suffered?" interjected Wells as he shot his hand out. "Name's Al, Allen Wells, and this is my cousin Taylor. We're on vacation."

Handshakes all around.

"My name's Bey. Ardeth Bey," the other returned. "But my friends just call me Ardie," he said cheerfully. "I'm here on vacation as well, although with all these people..."

"Kids never notice crowds," threw in Wells. "They'll have a good time no matter how many people are around."

"And *we* can have some time off... Taylor? Is that correct?" asked Ardie.

"Yeah. For me, time off from teaching math, anyway," he responded.

"And for me at least some time away from the drudgery of the bond market."

"Hey, this starts to sound like office talk," put in Wells. "Think I'll go back to the cabin and take a nap."

"I'll walk you to the elevator," offered Taylor.

The pair bid goodbye to their new friend and headed back to the elevator.

"You don't have to walk me all the way back," said Wells. "From here, it's all secure."

"If you say so."

"I do. Besides, I've got to check that piece of thread you left on the door."

Taylor chuckled. "Okay. See you later..."

"At dinner. Wear a nice coat," suggested Wells.

"Whatever you say," agreed Taylor.

The elevator doors opened, Wells got in, and in a moment, Taylor was standing there by himself.

He returned to the coffee bar just as Ardie was finishing his drink.

"You're back!" remarked the fellow.

"Yeah, can't fly on just one latte," he replied.

Ardie chuckled. "Well, enjoy it. I have to find my wife and daughter. Maybe I'll see you tomorrow."

"Yeah, maybe. Have a nice evening," he said as the man walked off.

"Uh, another latte, uh... Mike?" he ventured.

"Yep, Mike. Latte comin' right up, sir," replied the barista.

The coffee was made and set before him on the counter in a thrice. He took a good tug on the beverage and then set down the cup.

"There's nothing like a hot cup of coffee, is there?" an elderly voice put in from the other end of the bar.

Taylor turned to see an old man on the last stool. The guy looked to be in his eighties. He was dressed in a boxy gray suit with a maroon vest beneath and a matching bow tie. A cane was propped next to his leg against the bar.

"Yeah, nothing like it," agreed Taylor.

"You are not what you seem," remarked the old man with a smile and a distinctly German accent.

Taylor didn't react but maintained an unruffled smile.

"Who among us really is what we seem?" he returned. "You, for instance, seem a kindly old gentleman, but who knows what's in your past?"

The old man chuckled. "And if you ever taught math in your entire life, I'll eat my hat."

"You don't seem to have a hat."

"Metaphorically."

Taylor smiled more broadly. "Y'know, it's not polite to listen in on others' conversations."

The old man stood from his stool, and grabbed his cane with one hand and his coffee cup with the other. He took a couple of steps towards Taylor.

"I'm too old to worry about social conventions. Come," he said with a heavy German accent as he turned towards the starboard side of the ship. "We can sit and watch the sun as it heads for the horizon."

Taylor nodded agreement, grabbed his cup, and followed the old fellow to the promenade where tables, chairs, and lounges were set up and smoking was permitted. The pair found an empty table and sat looking out to the sea.

"If I'm not mistaken, I think you are probably a bodyguard for that Mr. Wells, are you not?" ventured the old man as he propped his cane against the wall behind him. "You needn't answer. I won't tell anyone," he added.

Taylor sat silently for a second. "You seem to assume a lot," he said finally.

The old man laughed. "No, no," he replied, "it's not an assumption, just an observation. I just noticed that you look around furtively as you both enjoy your drinks. You lead him to the elevator when he wants to go. Your body is not just fit but quite muscular, and you move with the supple agility of a cat. Isn't it obvious?" he reasoned.

"Or you may simply have a fertile imagination," Taylor suggested.

The old fellow chuckled to himself. "It's no matter. Look, I'm not here to expose you. You have to understand, at my age, about all the fun I can have is in observing people, and you represent a rather interesting case," he explained.

Taylor smiled back at the fellow. "And what about yourself?" he began. "I'm guessing you're in your nineties even though you look a bit younger. By your German accent it's no guess to imagine that you went through WWII—on the other side, of course. That thin gold band on your right hand indicates you were married in Germany and not in the west where we wear the band on the left hand. Also, that you're alone tells me that your wife has passed, probably some time ago. So, you must be here with children or grandchildren who want to keep grampa busy and vital. Meanwhile, your powers of observation tell me that you once had a job in law enforcement or... a position in the old Wehrmacht where you used your investigative acumen. Am I right?" Taylor ventured as he took a sip of his latte.

The old gentleman laughed. "Right on all counts, Mr. Holmes" he admitted. "My name's Ulrich Kaiser. I'm here with my grandchildren and a niece. They want to keep me moving and vertical for as long as possible. And you were also correct about my wife Adele, the love of my life, who died three years ago this month. Another reason the kids wanted to bring me to keep my mind off of it."

"And your military background?" asked Taylor.

"Nothing as nefarious as you may think. Yes, I was in the Kriegsmarine during the war. Actually joined before the war in '38 where I became a Matrosengefreiter—seaman, private first class. I was only fifteen at the time but lied about my age." He stopped. "By the way, do you mind if I smoke a cigar? My kids won't let me in their presence, and it's my only vice."

Taylor took another sip of his drink. "Go ahead. It's all right with me," he replied. After all, how many times had he been in the smoke-filed precincts of Marge's office or Harry's when he lit up?

Kaiser took out a hard, leather container from his suit pocket and extracted a cigar. "Cuban," he said as he produced a cutter with which he clipped the end before he snapped on his Colibri. He took a few puffs and then a long drag. Then he blew out the blue smoke luxuriantly.

"You were saying?" Taylor interrupted.

"Yes, I was in the navy. But it wasn't the military connection that attracted me. I just loved the sea. Anyway, I eventually worked my way up to Steuermannsmaat."

"That was quite a jump in rank, wasn't it?"

"Yes, but I was good at my job and saved my superior from making a mistake. He was grateful," he replied and then took another draw on his cigar and let the smoke issue into the salt-sea air.

Two middle-aged fat women who were passing wrinkled their faces disagreeably at the smoke, looked disapprovingly at the old man, fake coughed, and hurried off lest they become contaminated by the vile stench.

Kaiser chuckled as he watched them go. "People are always so concerned about what others do, and women are so quick to judge—not like my Adele. She was a gem," he observed with a gruff laugh.

Taylor chuckled along with him.

"Aber, what was I saying?" asked Kaiser as he scratched his balding head.

"You just joined the navy," Taylor put in.

The old man's eyes widened. "Ach, ja," he responded as he nodded. "But that was only the beginning of the tale."

"The tale?" repeated Taylor blankly.

"Jawohl. Something so unbelievable that even I who experienced it still have trouble believing that it actually happened," he responded excitedly as he tapped the end of the cigar into an ash tray.

Taylor grinned and moved a little closer to the old man.

"You have to understand," began Kaiser, "the whole thing was 'streng klassifiziert' for decades and decades, but I can tell you now, if you'd like to hear it. Even if you think I'm just ein alter Verrückter."

Taylor snorted a laugh. "Naw, I've known all kinds of people. You're not crazy. So, fire away," he charged him.

Ulrich Kaiser took a long drink of his coffee and another long drag off his cigar.

"So, it began in late '38 when I was a seaman on the *Schwabenland*," he began. "I'd only been in the service maybe zehn Monate. The Oberkommando ordered us out to sea, presumably to do some whaling as a way to obtain fats and oil for the Vaterland—in preparation of the coming war I expect, or at least that was the scuttlebutt on board ship, you understand."

Taylor nodded.

"But none of it was true," Kaiser went on with a rueful laugh as he took a long draw off his Cuban. "They lied to us. Alles gelogen! You see, what they really wanted us to do was..."

"Mister Taylor?" a voice suddenly interrupted.

The pair looked up to see that a fellow in white, dark epaulets on his shoulders, and a high-pressure cap placed squarely on his head was standing in front of them.

"Yes?" Taylor responded.

"Ah, Mr. Taylor," repeated the man with a cheery and melodious British accent and broad smile. "Chief Officer Palfrey, sir. Mr. Wells said I might find you down here. Sir, Captain Drake was wondering if he could prevail upon you to come to the bridge. It shouldn't take long, sir."

Taylor squinted at him. "To the bridge? Why?"

"I'm not sure, sir, but as I understand it, it has to do with a fellow passenger."

"Fellow passenger?"

Palfrey looked at a loss. "All I know is that the captain has assured me that your help would be greatly appreciated, sir, and that I was to communicate that to you."

Taylor took in a breath. "Very well," he replied and turned to Kaiser. "Perhaps we can pick up this conversation another time," Taylor ventured.

"Of, course," replied Kaiser, "I have all the time in the world, young man," he said as he took another long draw off his stogie which this time made the Chief Petty Officer cough and start walking away.

Palfrey led Taylor up an escalator and then forward to an elevator that required a security key. The two boarded and in a second had arrived at the bridge.

Taylor had always pictured in his mind an outdoor station with a man-sized, big honking ship's spoked helm on it where a grizzled, peg-legged old salt wearing a sou'wester with the brim up steered the ship with all sails unfurled—like they used to do on the old 19th century schooners. But that was pure romanticism. The bridge of the *Flying Cloud* was bright and modern with wraparound windows that formed a 180-degree arc. In fact, the space looked more like the inside of the Starship Enterprise being decked out with large command chairs, a phalanx of computer monitors all around, and about ten men working at them. Sadly, there was no grand ship's wheel.

"Officer of the Watch," belted out Palfrey. "Permission to enter the bridge."

"Permission granted," replied a man who was checking out the scenery with a large pair of binoculars.

Palfrey led Taylor across the space to an older man in starched whites with a matching white beard. He stood next to a pretty, young lady who looked to be in her early twenties. Palfrey removed his hat and saluted smartly.

"Mr. Taylor, this is Captain Drake," he said as the captain turned towards his new guest.

The bearded captain looked like Anthony Hopkins with a face deeply etched with lines from many years of bearing heavy responsibilities.

"Mr. Taylor..." said the man with the perfect clarity of a perfect British accent as he extended his hand.

Taylor shook the hand.

"Miss Young here is in some distress and would like to have a word with you. You can have your discussion in the restaurant on deck eleven."

―――――

"So the stewardess remembered that you'd been talking with him in the aisle, and it just took a little bit of work to find out who you were. Since just about everyone on the plane was scheduled to take this boat, that was how I found you," explained Miss Tabitha Young with misted eyes as she went over the details of her fiancé's unfortunate demise."

"When's the last time you ate?" asked Taylor.

"I can't remember," replied the lass.

"Then could I maybe get you a little something to eat or drink?"

She nodded. "maybe something light," she said.

Taylor waved over a waiter who was serving people in the "Galley"—one of the few eateries that was more like a restaurant and not just another "grab and go" stand of which the ship had many. The place was all decked out in faux wood and coarse-cut, lacquered spars with old-looking tables and captain's chairs set up to resemble the galley of a pirate ship. The waiters were dressed like buccaneers, and the menu boasted such enticing fare as kippers and grog next to the hamburgers, nachos, and milkshakes.

The waiter duly arrived, and Tabitha ordered some fries and a strawberry shake—cuisine that apparently represented the millennial's idea of wholesome nourishment. Taylor ordered a latte. The waiter wrote it down and quickly disappeared.

"You see," she said as she dabbed at her eyes with a Kleenex, "Bob and I were going to take this trip and then get married when we returned to Florida."

"Isn't that a bit turned around. Shouldn't the trip have been the honeymoon?" asked Taylor.

Tabitha, or rather "Tabby," as she preferred to be called, blanched a little.

"Bob and I have been living together for three years. I grew up with him in Asheville but we finally connected when he and I worked together at a Home Depot. We got engaged and moved to Florida where he got into business with an old friend—Martin, Martin Millner. Things have been going great for us, and we finally decided on getting married. Then this trip came up."

Taylor knitted his brow. "What kind of business?"

Her eyes widened and she took a breath. "Collectibles," she said. All kinds of collectibles: antiques, toys, cars—anything anybody would like to collect."

Taylor nodded. "And your trip?"

"It's quite simple; a business opportunity came up. Martin was going to stay at the office in town, and Bob was set to go. Since I was visiting family in Germany, we thought we'd make a fun trip out of it," she responded with a brief smile that cascaded into tears once she realized the incongruity of their plan and the reality of what had happened to her fiancé.

Taylor patted her on the shoulder. "Hey, buck up. Your fiancé seemed to be a very happy and positive person..."

"He was," she said, sniffing back tears.

"And I'm sure he wouldn't want you to suffer like this."

"I'm sorry, Mr. Taylor. I just can't help it."

It was difficult to determine whether the sorrow was real or all an act. He'd seen a lot of women pull off some very artful performances that would convince a jury they were preaching the gospel when they weren't. But what did it matter to him what this chick was saying? It wasn't his deal—none of it. He would have gone on thinking along these lines, but just then the waiter reappeared with their order.

"Eat," Taylor prodded. "The world always looks better when you get a little food in you."

With that, Tabby started in on her fries with intermittent sips of her shake. Taylor sipped at his latte and talked offhandedly about the wonders of the ship—as much as he'd read in the brochures, anyway—while she nodded and munched one fry after the other until the little red cardboard container they came in was as empty as the cup of pink stuff she'd drunk.

"Well, I guess I'd better go. I've taken up enough of your time," she said.

"Sorry I couldn't have helped more," he replied.

"No, no," she averred, "it did help to talk to you. Anyway, I'll be leaving the ship at our first port of call and going back home. I have a lot to do."

"Understand," replied Taylor as he stood.

She stood up and smiled a little. "Well, I hope you enjoy your trip Mr. Taylor," she said.

"Take care of yourself," he returned.

"I'll do my best," she replied and then walked off and out of the restaurant.

Taylor followed her with his eyes and then picked up his cup and took a final slug of java.

CHAPTER 3

It was getting to be late afternoon by the time he got back to his stateroom. But before he went in, he knocked at the adjoining door, and Mandy Bannon and her perky ponytail opened almost at once.

"Oh, I thought it might be Mrs. Wells," she said with surprise written all over her face.

"Nope. Just us chickens."

She chuckled.

"Just checking to see how you and the rug rats are doing."

"All present and accounted for," she replied. "They are both out for a nap. But... it's not your job to look after us," she added with a little shot of skeptical curiosity. "Or is it?"

"No, no," he returned defensively. "It's just that it's a big ship, the kids are a handful, and I..."

"No need to explain, Taylor," she returned easily. "Thanks for looking in on us."

"Well, all right then. See you at dinner."

"At dinner, then."

She closed the door and left him standing alone in the corridor.

Once inside his stateroom, Taylor checked his phone for any message from Wells. Seeing none, he flaked out on his bed as his mind re-ran the events of the day including his meeting with the old German and his interview with the girl. It didn't take long for him to fall into a nice, restful sleep.

It was dark outside when he awoke. He checked the clock on the nightstand. Time to get ready for dinner. He buzzed Wells, and they agreed that they'd all go together to the dining room. He threw on a sportscoat and was out the door in a second.

Wells had made a standing dinner reservation for a table in the grand dining room for the whole of the trip. It had a spectacular view across the starboard bow where at this time of the evening the stars twinkled in the distance and the moon reflected off the undulating waves. After they took their places, Wells ordered drinks all around: scotch for him, a mojito for the missus, chocolate shakes for the kids, tea for Miss Bannon, and a Coke for Taylor. Almost before they settled in, the libations were served in a thrice.

In fact, Taylor was not a little surprised to see Mrs. Wells actually conscious and dressed up for dinner—a little too dressed up to his way of thinking.

"Enjoying the trip so far?" he asked.

She took a long draw off the mojito and shot him a disinterested stare. "I don't like boats. I only came on this trip on the recommendation of friends to see the ports of call where we're stopping."

"Oh," he replied shortly.

"She goes for the shopping," Wells put in. "Some people go for the art, some for the culture. Me, I couldn't care less about that stuff. All that dead history. All those old dead artists, all those religious paintings. For what, I ask you. For what?"

"Maybe for the enlightenment of mankind," ventured Mandy.

Wells chuckled. "You're still young yet. All those great artists of the past... They all depended on patrons and on their money. Money. Show me a starving artist, and I'll show you a failure in life. What do you think, Taylor?" he queried.

"Me?" Taylor replied.

"Yes. About art," Mandy put in.

"Uh... I'm more at home teaching math. Art I leave to Pat Morgen who teaches in the classroom next to mine," he replied.

"Y'know, you don't strike me as a math teacher," stated Mandy with a curious look on her face. "I don't know what it is, but I can't see you doing that job."

"Me neither," returned Taylor. "My mother, Alan's Aunt Alice, always said I should go into advertising. She kept sending me clippings of jobs even after I got my credential," he added offhandedly. "Personally, I always kind of had a yen to go in for flying, but unfortunately I couldn't pass the medical exam due to a hearing problem I've had since I was a kid. So, I had to settle for the life of a desk jockey."

"How disappointing," the wife observed dryly.

Taylor firmed up his mouth. "Y'know, I was maybe disappointed when I started, but when you become a teacher there are rewards you can't put on a balance sheet. I mean, seeing a kid finally understand a math concept when the light goes on in his eye. Now that's something," he effused.

Mrs. Wells had a look of incredulity plastered on her face. "Whatever floats your boat," she returned dismissively and then turned to her husband. "Alan, can we finally get something to eat. I've had a hard day," she said with a pout.

Yeah, thought Taylor. All that sleeping and lounging around is apt to wipe you out.

"Yeah, yeah," Wells piped up. Then he raised his hand and waved over the waiter who was there in a second with one-page menus.

"Anyway," interjected Mandy, "while you're sightseeing, I'll take the children to a film and some of the other attractions and activities on the boat..."

"Ship," corrected Wells.

"Yes, ship," repeated Mandy with a little laugh. "There's all kinds of things for the kids to do, so have fun and don't worry."

At that moment, a tall man with a white beard who wore a white outfit with epaulets on the shoulders stepped up to the table.

"Good evening, I'm Captain Drake. I hope you're enjoying our cruise," he said as he gazed at each individual face by face.

Mrs. Wells perked up at the appearance of the captain's commanding presence. "Yes," she said with a little lilt in her voice. "Your accommodations are most comfortable."

The captain nodded. "We aim to please, ma'am," he replied in a tone dripping with confidence. "If you need anything at all, don't hesitate to contact our staff," he said and then turned and moved on to another table.

As the others chatted about the unexpected visit, Taylor watched the captain as he went from table to table finally sitting down at a table up front where, to his surprise, Miss Tabby Young sat as the captain's dinner guest—doubtless a result of her tale of woe.

Dinner over, Mr. Wells decided to hit the sack while his spouse wanted to see the rest of the ship and whatever nightlife there was to experience. For that, Wells asked Taylor to accompany her wherever she wished to go. Meanwhile, Mrs. Wells—Cassandra that is—invited Mandy to come along after the kids were tucked in.

"They'll be safe, won't they, Taylor?" she asked out of nowhere.

Taylor nodded. "Uh... in your stateroom? I'd certainly say so. Don't' you think so, Alan?" he asked his host."

"Yeah, sure," he replied. Besides, they'll be right near me," he opined.

"But I think first I'll get the children settled before I join you if you don't mind," said Mandy.

"Suit yourself," agreed Cassandra. "All right, then, let's get going," she pressed. With that she gave Alan a peck on the cheek and headed towards the Grand Salon with Taylor in tow. When they were clear of the family, Cassandra stopped and turned to Taylor.

"I think it's nice that you have this history with Alan—I mean from his youth."

"Why's that?"

"I've really only known Alan for eight years. I have no actual perspective on who he was as a kid."

"He was a great kid," Taylor faux reported. "Now, we really only connected at family get-togethers, on holiday, and at summer camp, but I can tell you, even then Alan was a straight shooter and a good guy."

"Huh. That's good to know."

"Why?

"Because when you marry someone, and particularly if they're older than you are as in our case, there's always that idea of the missing connections to the past that you can never understand."

"Unless you have a cousin to fill you in?"

Cassandra Wells laughed. "Good, that's good," she replied.

"Okay, let's see if we can't find a place on this tub where there's a little life and I can find something good to drink and maybe have a little adult fun." With that she turned and led Taylor off in another direction.

Maybe she wasn't such a bad egg after all he thought to himself as he followed her.

The ship was basically set up to take care of the needs of families and specifically for the enjoyment of kids. In that sense, it presented a veritable Disneyland of fun opportunities for the rug rats. There were two theaters where only G-rated movies and cartoons played continuously. On the same deck were arcades with all sorts of attractions. Little girls could become movie princesses while the boys could emulate pirates or space rangers. All that kind of stuff. But the adults were taken care of as well. There were nightclubs, salons, a pool for only the over-twenty set, and professional live stage productions of musicals, dramas, comedies, and whatever else would entertain parents when the kids were off getting their quantum of kid fun.

Taylor and Mrs. Wells eventually made it to the Club 21 Nightclub where there was drinking and a stand-up comic who told risqué but not too risqué jokes to the adults who could relax, buy booze, and get sloshed. Because these clubs served alcoholic drinks, they were the only places on the ship where one actually was required to use a credit card for payment. Otherwise, regular drinks on the ship were all free.

The pair found a table to watch the comic. Taylor ordered his usual latte, and Cassandra ordered a bottomless mojito—which meant that they would just keep filling the glass as long as she was there.

After about ten minutes, Taylor's phone went off. It was Mandy wanting to know where they were. After Taylor clued her in, the two went back to watching the comic who, it turned out, copied Rodney Dangerfield's hilarious patter to the delight of the crowd.

In another ten minutes, someone suddenly grabbed a chair and joined the duo. Taylor was taken aback for a moment. It was Mandy all right, but she looked really different.

"I know," she said with an apologetic pout, "I decided to wear my hair down. I hope it looks all right."

"All right" was something of an understatement. With the addition of a little make up, lipstick, and who knows what else women use to enhance their features, Amanda Bannon was actually dazzling. She smiled at Taylor in a way he found difficult to fathom.

"You don't mind?" she said.

"Not at all," he replied.

"Oh, brother," put in Cassandra acridly with an eye roll. She held up her empty glass and wiggled it at the waiter. "Another," she called out and the waiter nodded and went off to make another libation for the lady.

"The children nestled all snug in their beds?" she asked dryly.

"Yes, certainly," replied Mandy. "They're so sweet. I promised them they could go to the pool tomorrow and see a movie too."

"Wonderful," returned the mother unenthusiastically. "Do whatever you need to keep them out of trouble. Just see that they don't drown. Their father would freak and we'd be tied up in litigation for who knows how long."

Mandy frowned and was just about to say something when a man appeared at the table.

"Mr. Taylor," he said.

It was Chief Officer Palfrey who despite his usual unflappableness appeared a tad flappable nonetheless.

"Uh, the captain has asked if he couldn't speak with you, if you don't mind," he stated.

Cassandra perked up. "Could I join in as well?" she asked expectantly.

"'Fraid not, Madame. Perhaps next time," he declared. Cassandra drooped as Taylor rose from the table.

"I'll get back as quickly as possible," Taylor assured the pair. Enjoy the show."

"With that he was off with Palfrey to wherever he was being led which turned out to be on one of the lower decks on the starboard side of the ship. They arrived at their destination where two seaman stood guard and nodded when Palfrey arrived to let him and Taylor through. Twenty yards ahead Captain Drake turned to greet Taylor with a serious look on his face.

"Mr. Taylor. Since we have been apprised of your true background by Mr. Wells, I was hoping you might help us out with a problem we've encountered."

"Yes, certainly," replied Taylor brightly. "What is it?"

"This," replied Drake as he stepped aside.

And there it was.

Tabby Young was lying on the floor of the corridor, quite decidedly dead as dead can be.

CHAPTER 4

She lay scrunched against the bulkhead with her body twisted to one side and her arm over her head. She had a dull look on her face with her eyes wide open in surprise and her mouth agape. Her pretty party dress was spoiled by a large blotch of blood on the front as a result of the deep gash that ran around her lily-white throat. Meanwhile, the gore spilled out in a torrent of red that was all over the walkway.

Tabby Young had died in the worst way possible; that is, if there was ever a good way to go, which was doubtful.

"I can't tell you how dreadful this is," said the captain. "After the terrible news she received about her fiancé, I wanted to extend every courtesy to her. I thought she deserved at least that much. But now..." he added as he shook his head sadly.

While the captain spoke, Taylor's quick mind was scrutinizing every inch of the scene of the murder.

"Any cameras on this area?" he asked.

"Unfortunately, not here. There's never much traffic on this deck."

"Um," grunted Taylor. "All right, then could you have a photographer go over every millimeter of this area and get the pictures to me as soon as possible—eight by tens if you can handle it?" he queried.

"Certainly," replied the captain at once. "Do you want us to look for fingerprints?" he asked.

"Won't be any," replied Taylor. He pointed to a smudge on the bulkhead. "See that?" he queried.

"Yes," returned the captain.

"The assailant wore gloves. Also, he was right handed and was just under six feet tall. Do you have someplace where I can get a better look at her?"

The captain stared him in the eye a little surprised at Taylor's erudition.

"We have a morgue," he replied.

"That's good," said Taylor. "And one more thing," he went on.

"Which would be?"

"Please keep this section of the walkway off limits from that end down near that door to the opposite end where your guards were standing and keep everyone off of it until we can get a better look at it. There's still the possibility that we may be able to pick up some footprints maybe from stepping in the blood where it would be carried down the path."

"You think?" queried the captain.

Taylor smiled grimly as he stood erect and took a breath. "It is commonly but accurately understood, captain, that no one makes it down to the water's edge without leaving tracks in the sand."

As beautiful as the *Flying Cloud* was, and as light-hearted a venue it may have seemed for the vacationers on board with all its exciting attractions, it nevertheless maintained a real morgue for whatever unexpected misadventures might befall the crew or the guests. Gruesome as the idea was to have this kind of locus of death on board the ship, it was professionally acknowledged that just about every ocean liner was apt to experience at least a couple of deaths during any given cruise, usually from heart attacks or falls and such. But murder? No, murder was something quite different, something malevolent, something that didn't fit in with the intended fun happenings and day-to-day life on a cruise ship of this kind. And even after the murder would be reduced to a set of facts that the coroner could adduce, there was always the larger problem in this particular case: the murderer was still at large.

The morgue was as cool as death and quite reminiscent of Malcolm Pratt's coroner's office in downtown L.A., brightly lit and completely sterile. There were a couple of large cabinets on one wall filled with medical paraphernalia. On the opposite end of the room there were stainless-steel refrigerated vaults for the hapless guests who might need them. Finally, there was only one stainless-steel slab in the middle of the room instead of the half-dozen or so that one could roll around the room in Malcolm's department.

Tabitha Young lay on the slab under a bright light and with a coverlet over her body. Someone had had the good taste to close her eyes. Still, the gash in her neck was fully exposed and looked even more gruesome with the blood washed from it. It was quite clear that she had been grabbed from the back and cut with one stroke of a blade from left to right.

"It doesn't look like she put up much of a fight or fought at all," commented the ship's doctor in his proper British. Doctor Guy Wyndham-Smythe sounded and even looked like that old British actor Terry Thomas save for the fact that he had gray hair instead of Thomas' black mane. He even had the same gap between his two front teeth.

"Look, he-ear," he said as he raised the girl's left shoulder. "See those bruises? I'd say it looks like he grabbed her from the rear and held her tightly with his left hand so that he could cut her with a knife that he held in his right," he explained with a canny look in his eye as he pantomimed the attack.

Taylor nodded. "I think you're right, Doctor," he replied.

"Capital!" returned Wyndham-Smythe.

"Any other marks?" asked Taylor.

"Just the bruises on her shoulder and, of course, that ghastly incision on her neck."

Taylor nodded again. "Um, a powerful hand left those bruises," he said.

"My thinking exactly," agreed the doctor. "You know, old man, when I was younger I did a bit of detective work myself in Birmingham," he volunteered.

"Don't say."

"Indeed, it's true. So you see, I do have some little understanding of what you professional chaps are all about and what you're looking for."

Taylor smiled. "Once we get to port, the police will probably be grateful for whatever you can tell them."

"But I thought *you* were handling this case, as it were," said Wyndham-Smythe in a tone like a kid who's had his best toy taken from him.

"Actually, I'm already on another case—completely incognito. You understand, I can't afford to have my cover blown."

"Oh, I should say not!" exclaimed Wyndham-Smythe. "You can count on me in any way you might require."

"Thanks, Doctor," said Taylor as he patted the other man on the shoulder. "Fear not, I'll probably be getting in touch with you before you know it."

Wyndham-Smythe gave a little salute. "Here, here! I'll be at the ready whenever you need me."

"You happen to have a magnifying glass?" asked the detective.

With that, Taylor left the morgue and returned to the scene of the crime where they had set up bright work lights that spanned the whole area. He set to work and covered every inch of the walkway with the magnifying glass like a bloodhound but was stymied by the coarse, rubbery surface that was meant to keep people from slipping if it became wet and slick.

"Damn!" he muttered under his breath. Then he turned to one of the staff who was there to help him. "I'm turning in. You folks cover it one more time and see if you can find something I missed. I've got an early day tomorrow. I'll check with the captain in the morning."

"Yes, sir," replied the man.

Taylor handed him the magnifying glass, asked him to return it to Wyndham-Smythe, and walked off in the direction of his stateroom.

He entered his cabin and went straight for his phone where he quickly punched in a number.

"Marge?" he said. "This is Taylor."

"Like I can't read the name on the call?" she who must be obeyed replied. "Nice that you're callin' us poor folk from your hoity-toity Mediterranean cruise," she cracked.

"Now, cut it out. I'm in a situation. It's a murder," he returned.

"Our client?"

"No, no. It's something else I've run onto. The ship's captain asked me to look into it, and I said I would."

"Um," she grunted. "We gettin' paid for this?"

"Nope," he shot back. "Chalk it up to pro bono work. Good for our image."

Marge guffawed.

"Okay, okay. I get it. Nevertheless, I need some work done."

"Okay," she relented with a great sigh. "Since we're being big-hearted and all that…"

"Right. Okay, I need whatever you can get me on a Tabitha or Tabby Young from Asheville. That's in North Carolina."

"I know where it is. Geesch! That it?"

"No," he continued. "I also need whatever you've got on a Robert or maybe Bob Ross and a Martin Millner. Ross might be from North Carolina, but I don't know about Millner. What I do know is that they have a business together in Florida. Think you can work that up?"

"Hey, bub," Marge countered. "If I can't do it, nobody can."

"S'why I always ask the expert," he returned. "I owe you a box of doughnuts."

"Don't you dare," she replied thunderously, then added, "But if you do, I like the raspberry jelly kind."

"Deal. Call me when you've got something. And thanks. I appreciate it. So will the captain."

"Yer welcome. It's no biggie. Besides, don't forget, I'm on salary," she said and hung up.

Taylor grinned and then punched in another number.

"Hey," answered the sultry voice of Abby Hart on the other end of the line. "I was beginning to think you'd forgotten me."

"That's never going to happen."

"Better not. So, how's the trip so far?"

He sighed. "Well, the bodyguard job is fairly routine. The guy I'm watching is nice; you'd like him. The wife, not so much. A real pain. But the kids are cute."

"A cruise with you around the Mediterranean would be nice. Wouldn't you like that?"

"Yeah, if it wasn't over water. But I'm managing to hold up. Found a place where a guy named Mike makes a decent latte. The only downside to the trip so far is that there's been a murder on board, and the captain's asked for my help."

"I don't know how you get into these things."

"Just kind of happened. It's actually kind of a sad story. But don't worry. I'm only helping out on this thing, and I'll be careful."

There was a moment of silence on the line.

"Abby?"

"You'd better be careful; that's all I have to say."

"Okay, okay. I will, I will. Promise. But now I have to be going. Have an early wake up for our first port of call."

"Call me again?"

"Of course. After I've got something new to tell you."

"All right. And I'll keep busy."

"Me too," he returned.

Abby rang off and he clicked off his phone. It was already pretty late. He tossed the cell phone onto the nightstand and got ready for bed. Before he closed his eyes, he stared at the ceiling and said "six-fifteen" out loud. Then he sacked out.

Morning arrived and Taylor awoke with a start. He looked at the clock on the bedstand: 6:15, it read. As he sat up, the alarm went off. He got out of bed to get the day going.

His first stop was the breakfast café buffet. He got himself a plate of eggs, sausage and an English muffin with jam. Surprisingly enough, they also served latte which he eagerly took as well. He picked a table where he sat alone with Alan's itinerary on his phone and perused a guide book while he ate. He also scratched a couple of names on the inside cover—guys he knew from the old days who lived in the area and who could help him if he needed help. Then he made his way to the bridge.

Captain Drake was already at work with Palfrey and his crew mapping out the duties of the day. Taylor reported what he found—or rather didn't find—and repeated that he was looking into the background of Tabby and her fiancé. He'd keep him apprised when he learned something new. The captain then reported that they definitely had no video of the attack or of anything in that sector of the ship. Moreover, whoever the murderer was, he apparently was on the ship legitimately. The captain had had the crew check out each guest's identity card—the one each person received when they boarded the ship—and they all checked out. There were no stowaways on board. At least that was something. The only other thing he had to report was that the French authorities had been contacted, and they were coming on board to investigate and take possession of the body while the ship made its regular stop at Nice.

"My very next venue," returned Taylor.

"Have a nice day. We've staying until after sundown for this leg of the journey."

"Will do," replied Taylor. "See you when I get back."

Taylor then went directly to Alan's stateroom to pick up his client and the wife. The three of them gathered the kids and Mandy and went for a short breakfast. Taylor only drank his latte. Then the parents kissed the kids, and Taylor, Alan, and Cassandra headed for their ride into town.

"Ride" was one way to say it. Actually, their ride was a speedboat that Alan had arranged for as opposed to the rest of the ship's passengers who had to be content grabbing the shuttles which would take them to the docks. Once there, Alan also had a limo pick them up to go wherever they wished, and wherever they wished to go was essentially where Cassandra wished to go. She wanted to see Nice, go for a stroll on the *Promenade des Anglais*, hit the *haut couture* joints, walk on the beach, and then motor from there to Monaco on the same road on which Grace Kelly drove in *To Catch a Thief* with Cary Grant. Once there she wanted to see the Prince's Palace, do a little gambling at the Casino and a little sunbathing on the private beach at Larvotto where they could also get a nice *salade niçoise* among other tasty delights at the redoubtable Monte-Carlo Sporting Club.

By late afternoon the limo had made the complete round trip after their tour which had gone off without a hitch. The couple was simply tired from just traveling while Taylor was even more tired from having to scan every group and individual to avert danger, although on this day there was none.

Having eaten sumptuously at the Sporting Club, Alan and Cassandra did not need a dinner and decided instead to hit the sack early. Taylor, meanwhile, dutifully undertook his final chore and went to check on the kids.

Mandy opened the door with a smile.

"You got sunburned," she observed.

Taylor laughed. "I also got quite a full day as we raced from Nice to Monaco and visited all the spots in between."

Mandy laughed.

"So how are the kids," he asked.

"Fine, just fine. Took them to see some cartoons, they played with some Star Wars stuff, and they went swimming which wiped them out. They're already asleep."

"That all?"

"No. Curtis want's a lightsaber, and Amy wants a doll. I told them they'd have to ask their parents."

Taylor laughed. "That's great. All right, I think I'll..."

"Would you like to get a cup of coffee?" she asked suddenly. "I'll buy you a latte. I mean, it's only seven o'clock," she ventured.

Taylor thought for a second. What could it hurt, he said to himself. "Sure," he answered. "Let me just get freshened up and changed, and I'll be right back."

Once in his cabin he checked his phone. No calls or mails from Marge—a fact he passed on to Palfrey who would in turn pass it on to the captain. Palfrey also reported that the French authorities had come aboard to investigate the murder and took Miss Young with them when they left. They would apprise the captain if they found anything. Thus, by the end of the day, it looked like Taylor, the captain, and the French authorities were zero for zero.

Mandy Bannon closed the doors behind her and joined Taylor in the corridor with a big smile on her face.

"Did you eat dinner?" he asked.

"No. I was waiting for the family."

"You needn't have. We all had a big lunch and they decided to go to bed early. But it would be unfair if you weren't able to dine. C'mon, our table awaits. I might also have a little something to eat at that."

The dining room was filled with the usual crowd except that the Wells family was missing and their table empty. Taylor and Mandy took their seats, and the waiter handed them their menus and left a basket of rolls with butter. Tonight the chef featured creamy herb grilled salmon and asparagus with a bed of toasted garlic rice. It looked good, and although Taylor had had a lunch of salad and fruit, this meal looked light enough that it wouldn't crimp his digestion. They both ordered it with water for her and a Coke for him.

"So how *was* the excursion?" asked Mandy as she buttered a sourdough roll from the bread basket.

"We mostly went to the places Cassandra wanted to see. It was actually fun, and for me better to be on land than near the water."

"What's wrong with water?"

"Aah. Had an accident as a kid. Almost drowned."

"When you and cousin Alan were at camp?"

"No, it was at another time. Alan didn't have anything to do with it."

"Funny, I can't see you drowning or being afraid of anything. I also can't see you teaching a math class to twelve year-old middle-school kids in Florida."

"Palm Beach, Florida, actually. Conniston Public Middle School, near Jupiter Florida where Taylor Swift lives in her big white mansion. I teach basic math up to geometry, five classes a day Monday through Friday with holidays and three months off in summer, although I also sometimes teach summer school."

"Really?" she returned skeptically.

"Hey, would I lie to you unless I absolutely had to?" he asked barefaced.

She laughed. "Okay, I believe you," she finally relented.

"And you?" he asked.

"Grew up in Burbank."

"I thought Burbank was a myth," he interjected.

She chuckled again. "No, it's a real place. Went to elementary through high school there. John Burroughs High where Ron Howard and Rene Russo attended. Grew up on Naomi street, plunk in the middle of the city."

Taylor raised his eyebrows. "Really," he returned.

"Yeah. Then went to UCLA and got a Master's in Education."

"A Master's. Why aren't you teaching at a college somewhere? What are you doing babysitting Wells' kids?"

Mandy chuckled at his questions. "Actually, I'm more of a tutor to these kids. Because of all of the disgustingly sick sex and race stuff they're pushing on little kids in public schools, Wells' kids are being home-schooled. Besides, the pay beats lots of jobs out there. More than that, I'm free to do as I like. I'm not at the mercy of creepy school administrators or the woke Department of Education. But I can easily imagine that you'd know firsthand about all that garbage, not to preach to the choir."

Taylor nodded. "I know just what you mean. That sounds like..." he was just saying when the waiter returned with their meals.

"Ah. Looks like it's time to eat," he declared.

Mandy Bannon was sincere, honest, and easy to talk to. Taylor was even disturbed that he was forced to make up stories to tell her; on the other hand, it wasn't his call—it was part of the job. Still, it was the first time he felt relaxed on the job. The first time he felt comfortable since the last time he saw Abby. And then his phone went off.

It was Wells. Taylor explained where he and Mandy were, and Wells told him that he, the missus, and the kids would be right down to join them. He told Taylor not to worry about his safety on the way. It'd be okay. He didn't think anyone on board was after him. With that he rang off.

"So much for off-duty chatter," he explained to Mandy. "The fam woke up and is coming down for dinner."

"Maybe we still have time for dessert, you think?" she ventured.

Taylor laughed but behind that kept thinking about what had happened to Tabitha Young. He hadn't heard anything from Marge yet, and it appeared he'd have to wait to see if she found anything because with the family coming down to join them, this evening looked to be a long one.

And so it was.

The Welles all came to dinner, but it was obvious that they were all still wiped out from the activities of the day. Worse yet, tomorrow the ship would be docking at La Spezia and from there they'd drive to Florence about two hours away. Then it'd be a day of seeing all the sights in the city; Michelangelo's David, Brunelleschi's dome, the Uffizi Gallery, the Medici Chapel, yadda, yadda, yadda. By tomorrow night they'd be wiped out again. The kids would again stay with Mandy and catch the kid entertainment venues on the ship which were nearly inexhaustible. Taylor was tired just thinking about it, but tired or not, this is what he was getting paid for. At least the food was first class he had to admit. The Welles decided to hit the sack right after they ate. Mandy also put the kids to bed after she got them ready and read them a nice fairytale.

Taylor was the last into his stateroom after he felt comfortable that everything and everyone was secure. He was about to take a shower when his phone began buzzing. He picked it up and sat on the bed. Marge had left him a message that she e-mailed him the information he was looking for.

He opened the document and began reading. After getting through less than half the thing, he suddenly stopped.

"What?!" he exclaimed aloud.

He instantly started punching numbers into his phone. After about ten rings, she finally picked up.

"Pierce Investigations," answered Marge.

"This is Taylor..."

"Yeah, I sent you the information like you asked. So?"

"Yeah, you did. I was just..."

"No, *I* was just going to lunch. So why don't you call me after..."

"Marge," he said forcefully, "this is important."

There was a brief silence. "Okay, so whaddaya want? But make it quick. I got a date with the mister," she relented.

Taylor took a breath. "All I want to do is re-check some of what you've got here."

"Hey, It took me a full day to run that stuff down. If you don't believe..."

"No, no. I trust what you did. I've just got to make sure about something."

"About what?"

"The girl. Tabitha Young."

"Like I told you. Born in Asheville, North Carolina. Parents both deceased. Has one sister."

"And her name again?"

"The sister? Uhh, lemme check again," she replied and then took a few seconds looking up the information.

"Yeah, here it is," she said coming back on the line. "Brooke Young. Also born in Asheville but moved to Durham where she lived for two years until she moved to Los Angeles three years ago. Got married to a rich guy in Brentwood where she still lives."

"And what is her married name?"

"Uh... that would be..." mumbled Marge as she scanned the records. "Uh, yeah, that would be Cameron. Her married name's Brooke Cameron. Whoa! Is that the same woman I spoke with who hired you?" she asked brightly.

"Yeah, it is. That's what I needed to know."

"What a coincidence."

"Yeah, isn't it. Anyway, thanks. Thanks a lot," he replied thoughtfully with a dark tone to his voice.

"Great. I'm still working on the Millner guy and their business. I'll write when I have something. Anyway, don't forget to bring me back something Italian and romantic," said Marge as she then rang off.

"But Taylor wasn't thinking about anything Italian or romantic. He was thinking about the dead girl in Bungalow Number 5 at the Beverly Hills Hotel and just how in the hell she was connected to the murder of her sister on the high seas.

CHAPTER 5

Taylor had a lot to think about. On the one hand, he had this gig protecting Alan Wells and family. On the other hand, there was the murder of Brooke Cameron and now her sister Tabitha Young. He stared blankly at a wall. What the heck was going on?

He momentarily mentally berated himself that he couldn't think this through as he usually did when he was back home in L.A. There he got a lot of his thinking done as he tooled around on the freeways. He hated to admit it, but the slow traffic patterns and delays gave him time to work out various scenarios concerning the crimes he dealt with. This time, however, he didn't have that luxury. He grabbed his phone again and punched in a number on his speed dial.

"Lieutenant Mott," came the terse announcement, but this time it was the man and not the outgoing message.

"Hey, it's Taylor."

"Well, well, well. Mr. Taylor of the upper crust set who's on a luxury cruise enjoying the delights of the Amalfi Coast and the beauties of Greece, I don't doubt."

"Something like that. But it's still a job, Theo," he shot back. "Anyway, it's not why I called you. You got a second?"

"Yeah, sure. A second I got. So why *did* you call? Getting tired of the Frutti de Mare, the Italian gnocchi, the tiramisu?"

"Actually, now that you've mentioned it, I think I've grown to like tiramisu. But what I've called you about is real business—your Brooke Cameron case."

"The Cameron case? What about it?" came a slightly skeptical-sounding reply.

"Apparently, Brooke Cameron had a sister."

"A sister? Really."

"Yeah, named Tabitha Young... and *had* is the operative term. I met her through some circuitous circumstances that are too long to get into. Anyway, the important thing is that a mere day after I met her, she was murdered."

"You're kidding. Murdered? Murdered how?"

"Slit throat."

"Ugh! Messy."

"As opposed to her sister's gruesome death, this one didn't look like anything personal—more like a professional hit. The guy didn't leave a single clue except that he's right-handed. Used gloves, was careful to avoid leaving any tracks; the whole nine yards. The only thing I'm sure of is that he's a passenger on this boat."

Mott was silent, apparently thinking through the problem for a moment.

"Mott, you still there?" pressed Taylor.

"Yeah, yeah I'm still here..." Mott returned thoughtfully. "Tell me," he went on, "does your current assignment have anything to do with this girl?"

"That's the thing; it doesn't. Anyway, I don't think so," Taylor replied. "This looks like a coincidence; that is, if you believe in coincidences. See, I ran into her fiancé getting on the plane in Florida. He was supposed to join her on the ship for some sort of holiday, but he apparently died during the flight. Now, I didn't hear of any foul play. Stuff like that, heart attacks, strokes, happens all the time, so I didn't make any connection."

"And then the girl was murdered," stated Mott.

"And then the girl was murdered. Yeah, it was..." but Taylor inexplicably stopped himself short.

"Y'know, I'd be on my toes if I were you," pressed Mott.

"I always am," Taylor shot back.

"Okay, you seem invested in this thing, so tell you what; I'll look into the fiancé. What's his name?"

"Uh... Bob or Robert Ross, possibly originally from Asheville, North Carolina. And he has a business in South Florida with a partner named Millner—Martin Millner. From what I gather, they were into some sort of collection business—antiques, that sort of thing. Marge at my office is looking into it. She's still gathering information. But with the number of resources you have at your disposal, you ought to be able to do a lot better."

"I'd like to think so. Anyway... Ross and Millner. Okay, I'll check all this out. And, by the way, if you need any help, just send me a ticket, and I'll be there before you know it," Mott added jocularly.

Taylor chuckled. "Deal! I'll even buy you a nice slice of tiramisu if you do," he agreed and rang off. Then he punched in another number.

"Chief Officer Palfrey here," came the reply.

"Palfrey, this is Taylor. I'm just checking in."

"Yes, sir," replied the Chief Officer crisply. "The French constabulary came on board this morning—four members strong—after the guests departed for their tours."

"They find anything?"

"Not that they shared with us, sir. And I must say, they were very thorough. They went over every inch of the murder scene but apparently, like you, came up empty. They also went over videos from our closed-circuit system that we had and took copies with them. We also gave them access to our ID system to see if they could identify anyone or perhaps find some miscreant who had mixed himself in among our passengers. Finally, they took the body of the young lady to see if there was anything else there to be found. Our ship's doctor, Doctor Wyndham-Smythe, accompanied them in case there was any other information to be shared," he stated.

"Excellent, Chief Officer," replied Taylor. "Then I'll await any other information they may provide. Meanwhile, you may inform Captain Drake that I have the authorities stateside working on this case as well."

"Thank you, sir. I will so inform the captain. Good night," replied Palfrey and hung up.

Taylor tossed his phone on the nightstand, reclined on his bed, and laced his hands behind his head, looking up at the ceiling. In his mind the idea of sheer coincidence already was gnawing at his better judgment like a rat in a cookie factory, and he couldn't shake the feeling that something was off.

The next day went just as expected. The ship docked at La Spezia which looked like an industrial port filled with containers and gantries more meant for cargo ships than luxury liners. Still, Wells' limo was waiting to whisk the group to Florence, the next Italian venue on the itinerary.

Taylor stayed close to Wells as he continually scanned the crowds and locales from behind his ray-bans. To the uninitiated, this might seem a relatively easy job. But, in fact, it was quite taxing because it required being on alert every second of the day for whatever might happen. At least an actual attack by someone would allow him some physical activity; on the other hand, it was of course better if everything remained copesetic—just like Madame Cassandra preferred.

As the afternoon waned away, it was time to get back to the ship, to the kids, to dinner, and to an early bedtime. On their return, Taylor was amused to see that Mandy looked as wiped out as Wells and his wife, and she hadn't even left the ship. Watching kids, he decided, was at least as taxing as what he was employed to do.

Since the parents had spent the entire day away, they decided not to go to the dining room but rather to have dinner in their stateroom and to watch a movie on the TV with the kids. Taylor and Mandy were off for the evening which, for Taylor at least, was something of a relief. Still, he planned to eat a solitary dinner in the dining room. To that end, he took a quick shower and threw on his evening duds. In a short time, he was sitting alone at the Wells' reserved table.

Tonight he had a choice of entrees and picked the rib eye steak done medium with steak fries, asparagus, and a Coke. While the waiter was getting his grub, he took out his phone to look over the itinerary in order to re-check the safeguards he'd planned even before they started the vacation. Apparently, tomorrow the ship would dock at the port city of Civitavecchia, yet another container port which was about an hour's drive from Rome. However, Casandra had decided not to go to Rome 1) because she'd already been there a couple of times in the past, and 2) because she found the town just an über-busy place where it was always too hot and a drag to negotiate through traffic. Instead, she and Wells decided to stay on board, maybe sit around the pool or do other stuff together with the kids. At night there were a host of events, films, and other venues on the ship to visit for the kids as well as for the adults that were a lot more accessible than anything in Rome. The ship's so-called

Grand Theater, in fact, was featuring a live version of *Annie* that both age groups could appreciate. Sure, *Annie* didn't make the hit list on Taylor's bill of fare, but fortunately a coffee bar was just around the corner from the theater, and Wells always had his phone handy if he needed him. Taylor had already checked out the place. The theater had one entrance and four exits, but Taylor had prepped Wells in advance exactly where to sit and what to watch for since even Wells—as much as he prized Taylor's surveillance—still desired at least a little freedom from constantly being protected if that was at all possible. In fact, certain venues on the ship like the theater indeed made it possible.

Assassination. That was the name of the game in which Alan and Taylor were involved. See, killing someone outright doesn't take much imagination or involved planning. If all you wanted to do is kill someone, you need only to single them out and put a bullet through their noggin. Simple, quick, clean. The real trick, however, is how to get away with it, and in most cases how *not* to involve those who ordered the hit. Again, those footprints that always lead to the water's edge. A hit done sloppily can easily backfire badly and had done so more times than you could count. Even the redoubtable KGB—now called the SVR—which had assassinated more people than you could shake a pierogi at got caught red-handed in the end numerous times because they left traces of one sort or other. For example, a couple of years back they were dumb enough to poison that Litvinenko defector in England who was given a drink laced with polonium-210. It was a horrible death and glaringly obvious who killed him once the authorities found the means. I mean, who the hell uses polonium-210! Only the Russians.

The CIA tried similar tricks by using stuff like ricin, nerve agent VX, and Botox. Ricin comes from the castor oil plant and is really deadly. It's also very versatile; that is, you can inject it or put it in food or drink. In the seventies the KGB nicked a guy named Markov in the leg with it, and he died. The problem was, however, that it took a few days for the guy to die, and it's traceable. Also, rumor some years back was that the CIA had even tried to eighty-six Castro with the stuff, but that didn't work out, and Castro died an old man.

Botox is a botulism toxin—the same one responsible for food poisoning. It is also a neurotoxic protein that can block the transmission of signals by the nerve cells and result in a paralysis of the vegetative nerve system leading to muscle weakness. In fact, just a few micrograms of Botox can be fatal if used for that purpose.

As far as the nerve agent VX is concerned, Kim Jong Un apparently had his half-brother knocked off by two women who sprayed the stuff right in his face at the airport in Kuala Lumpur. VX is the most dangerous known chemical nerve agent known. Just 0.4 milligrams of the stuff is enough to kill an adult. That's equivalent to just a couple grains of salt... and, of course, it's traceable.

BTX (Batrachotoxin), another neuro toxin would probably be the most successful agent to use for a professional hit; that is, if you could get it. See, it's produced by the poison dart frog of South America, and in order to make it you'd have to have at least a thousand such frogs. Trouble is, they only produce the toxin in the wilds of the jungle, not in captivity. Nevertheless, the poison is particularly desirable since its effects mimic heart arrhythmia and ventricular fibrillation which would result in cardiac arrest. And cardiac arrest—hey, it could happen to anyone, right? For that reason plus the fact that the toxin dissipates quickly, in most instances, the event would be case closed; death by natural causes. It also would be fairly easy to administer to the victim, probably best by injection. You'd just have to walk by the victim and quickly inject them. They'd hardly notice it. However, if the injection site is located post mortem due to redness or swelling, well then, suspicion would probably run high that this death was not quite kosher and an investigation would certainly ensue because investigators aren't idiots and absolutely *would* notice even if no one else did.

As Taylor was running these peregrinations through his tired skull, he became aware that someone was standing next to him.

"Ach, Mr. Taylor," the man said in a comfy old-guy German accent worthy of an aged Ludwig Stossel.

Taylor looked up to see the old gentleman he'd met at the coffee bar who was now leaning on his cane next to the table. Taylor smiled.

"Ah, yes... Mr. Kaiser, if I'm not mistaken."

The old man beamed. "Ja, ja. Ach, you did not forget. Not being forgotten means a lot to an old man."

"Nonsense," replied Taylor. "As I recall, you were telling me a very interesting story of the days in your youth as a seaman."

Kaiser beamed again and chuckled. "And I promise to tell you the end of that tale the very next time we share Kaffee together," he pledged. "It is astounding. But right now, my family is waiting for me for dinner," he added as he pointed to a table across the room. "So, till then, Auf Wiedersehen."

"Ja, bis später," replied Taylor in his best Deutsch as the old man sauntered off across the room.

"Friend of yours?" inquired a female voice suddenly. Taylor turned to see Mandy Bannon seating herself at the table.

"I thought you'd certainly be knocked out from your day with the kiddies," he ventured as she slipped off her sweater and put her bag on the chair next to her.

Mandy laughed. "Knocked out or not, I still need some sustenance to get me through the next day since we're staying on board," she replied with a chuckle. "So what's it like out there in the big world?" she asked.

"Where we are now? Very Italian. Everything made with olive oil and red wine under a hot sun with a gazillion other tourists," he replied.

She took a great breath. "Yeah, tourists. Still, much as I love these kids, it might be fun to be free to see the sights."

"Well, we'll be hitting Greece at the end of the cruise—Athens and Mykonos. Wait for that. I think Wells will give you time to look around."

"Yeah, that would be nice," she replied as she grabbed the menu. "So what did you order?"

"I got the rib-eye steak with the asparagus. And a Coke."

"A Coke," she repeated. "Of course. Coke is based in Florida, isn't it?"

"In Georgia. Atlanta," he corrected. "Florida's famous for fun-ride parks, the Florida Keys, alligators, and currently, python hunts. But pythons aside, Coke's in Atlanta. Actually, I get the feeling you already knew that."

Mandy smiled cryptically to herself. "You know, I think I'll have the salmon steak with the wild rice, sautéed vegetables, and a glass of rosé," she announced brightly.

"Sounds like an excellent choice," he replied and waved over the waiter who duly took her order and disappeared.

"So who was the old gentleman you were talking to?" she asked.

"You mean Mr. Kaiser? I met him at the coffee kiosk the first day we were on the ship. We struck up a conversation and he started to tell me about his youth in the navy. A cruise will bring that sort of thing out of people. You know, camaraderie on board."

"No, I didn't," she replied. "How about you? Do you like cruises?"

"Me?" he returned. "As I think I explained, I don't like water very much from an accident I had as a kid," he admitted. "I only came along because Alan was afraid that after Cassandra would drag him through museum after museum and a bunch of shops, he'd get bored to tears. Besides, it was a free trip to places I've never visited."

"Has he... gotten bored to tears that is?"

"Not as long as he has someone to talk to."

"No doubt about integers, square roots, and common denominators I suppose," she cracked.

"You're pretty funny," he shot back, catching her drift. "Naw, we have more in common than that. But hey, don't sell Alan short. There's all kinds of stuff going on out there in politics, the stock market, and in world news in general. Alan and I can go over that stuff all day long while Cassandra's checking out her umpteenth Rubens or buying junk from the shops."

"My, my. You seem to have an answer for everything," she reflected apropos his rapid-fire responses.

"You would too, particularly if you have to stand in the front of a room full of teenagers five times a day who want to ask you about anything other than what the class is about."

Mandy laughed laced with the exhaustion from her day of toil. "I'm sorry if I seem to be prying," she said. "It's just that you as a school teacher seems so incongruent an idea. It just strikes me that way," she admitted.

"Actually, my mother also could never see me as a school teacher either. She used to send me article upon article about getting into business like Alan did. So in that respect, I guess you're on the right track," he put in jocularly.

At that point the waiter returned with both their orders, and they began to work their way through their meals with intermittent small talk. Once they had finished, Taylor suggested a walk on deck to give them time to digest their meals.

It was a balmy, starry Mediterranean night of the kind you only find written about in novels; yet, it was all real. The sky was a canopy of bright-white dots with a full moon illuminating a sparkling sea below as the salt-sea air filled one's lungs. And unlike during the daytime when everything on board seemed rushed and loud, the evening was mellow. The music of a mandolin played somewhere while lots of guests walked along the promenade or sat in the lounges simply enjoying the night.

"Are you married or engaged?" Mandy asked suddenly, which took Taylor by surprise.

"Uh... no to both questions," he answered. "You?"

"No," she replied.

"I mean, who has time for serious relationships!" he retorted. "The only person I've sort of dated sporadically in the last couple of years is Margaret Pepper—our school's registrar. But she's just a... just a buddy. Nice lady. Comes from Maine and a long family line. Visited her folks once. They own one of those cabins—camps they call them—on one of those lakes in Maine."

"Sounds, cozy," she returned.

"If you like that sort of thing and the gigantic mosquitos that go along with it in the summer, I guess. Say, would you care for a little dessert?" he suddenly asked out of nowhere.

Mandy hesitated a second. "No, it's been a long day. I think I'm going to turn in if you don't mind. We'll do it another time," she replied. "Good night," she said and walked in the opposite direction back towards her stateroom.

Taylor took a breath. "Uh, dodged a bullet there," he said to himself and then headed for the coffee kiosk.

Once there he ordered his latte and sat back thinking over the events of the day like he always did back home at Barney's. It was nice having all his little chickens safe in their roosts, and he didn't have to worry about them, especially with this pall of death that Tabitha's demise had suddenly thrust upon him. Thank God Abby wasn't here, he thought.

Brooke Cameron and Tabitha Young. Sisters. Why didn't he notice a similarity right off, he asked himself. And both murdered in so short a space of time. It couldn't be coincidence, but he was missing the pieces to pull this thing together. He'd just have to wait for some other piece of evidence to show up, he decided. With that he gulped the rest of his latte and headed back to his cabin. Tomorrow would be another long day.

As Taylor made his way to the elevator, he didn't notice the dark figure shadowing him.

It took him no time at all to get ready for bed. He remarked to himself that he was even getting used to the mattress, so maybe he'd sleep better tonight. He chuckled to himself. "Margaret Pepper." Where'd the hell did he get that from? Some ghost from back in the day or an old teacher, he guessed. Too funny. Anyway, now it was time to rest up. He could laugh about it more in the morning.

It was a little after three in the morning. It was quiet on the ship save for the "Woosh" sound that the waves made as the bow of the ship sliced through them.

Taylor lay asleep in his bed when he suddenly woke with a start. The pressure in the room had changed. Then he perceived the sound of the ocean and an inflow of sea air.

Without thinking, he thrust his hand up just in time to catch and deflect someone's wrist that was covered in rubber.

"Thwack!" went the sound of something striking the headboard of the bed next to his head as he spun around on his back and kicked the assailant in the ribs. The guy gave a short grunt and struck Taylor in the jaw with his fist as he sat up. But Taylor then sprung to his feet and kicked the man in the head causing him to stumble backwards towards the exterior sliding door. As Taylor jumped from the bed to the floor to catch the guy, he had already vanished out the door. Taylor ran after him, but the man had disappeared around the bulwark that separated his veranda from his neighbor's towards the stern of the ship.

At once there was a knocking at the door.

When he opened it, there stood Mandy.

"What happened?" she asked. "I heard a loud crash."

Taylor smiled as best he could under the circumstances. "Uh, I'm sorry, I'm not used to the ship or the new mattress, and I guess I fell out of bed and knocked over the lamp," he explained gamely.

"You fell out of bed?"

"Yeah. Flat on my kisser. Dumb, huh!"

"Yes, your face is red."

"Where I fell on it. But don't worry, I'm okay," he said.

Mandy wrinkled her forehead. "Well... all right. If you say so."

"I say so," he reassured her. "Now get to bed and I'll try real hard not to fall out of bed again."

At that she smiled a little skeptically but went on her way.

Taylor returned to the veranda, looked out, and shut and locked the sliding door. Then he went to the bed and switched on the light. The rooms were supposed to be sound proof which meant that they weren't as sound proof as advertised or Mandy simply had exceptional hearing.

"Hm!" he grunted as he then beheld what his nocturnal visitor had left him.

"It was a seventeen-inch long saw-blade bowie knife with a metal guard, wooden handle, and a metal pommel. It had been stuck solidly into Taylor's headboard with great force maybe two inches or so deep next to his head; the rest of it jutted out into the room as a message of death.

Chief Officer Palfrey, Captain Drake, and Doctor Wyndham-Smythe arrived together after Taylor rang them up and explained the circumstances. Since the ruckus was detectable in the kids' stateroom next door, Taylor cautioned them to be as quiet as they could be lest it awaken the others and particularly Mandy once again.

They all checked Taylor's room over, but apart from the bowie knife in the headboard, there didn't appear to be any fingerprints since Taylor explained the man had been wearing rubber gloves. There were also no marks on the door which apparently had been jimmied with a thin edged tool of some kind. And since Taylor thought the exterior steel bulkheads at either end of his veranda provided sufficient security, he hadn't thought to latch the actual lock. That made entry to the cabin easy. "Hard cheese, old man," volunteered Wyndham-Smythe. Taylor decided that he wouldn't do that again.

In fact, Palfrey had to twist the knife a little to remove it from its wooden target and wrap it in a towel for fingerprinting. Thereupon, the trio of officials silently left Taylor to the remainder of his evening with the jagged rent in his headboard.

Morning meant breakfast, and Wells' entourage met together to get their marching orders.

The mother and father had decided to spend the day with little Amy and Curtis by the pool and then go to some of the entertainments that the kids liked. Mandy could hang around with them or go ashore. Mandy picked the latter option and provided the parents with a list of the best things for them and the kids to see. Taylor, on the other hand, "volunteered" to stay close by even though Mandy had suggested they see a little of the Italian life ashore together. She was a little disappointed that he didn't take her up on her offer, but he lessened the pain by offering to free her up by watching the kids while the parents were doing other things. Of course, she didn't know that sticking near Alan actually was a job he was getting paid to do. At length she decided to accompany a couple of women she'd gotten acquainted with playing Mexican Train Dominos and Mahjong while watching the kids during the day. Two of the women were really special. Anna was a dental hygienist from Austin, Texas who was unattached and was taking her vacation on this cruise because she wanted to see the Greek isles. Casey was also single and was taking the cruise alone since she got stood up by her fiancé who had to stay home because of his job. It was doubly disappointing because they'd saved for this trip for two years, and then he got the news that he had to complete a project for his firm. Since they couldn't see an opportunity to travel any time in the near or even distant future, the two decided that Casey shouldn't waste the chance now. They cashed in his ticket so she could use the money any way she wished, and she took the cruise. She called Mark at home every day so that he could at least experience the trip second hand. Anyway, none of the three women had ever seen Rome before.

And so it was that Taylor and the Welles parked near the pool with the kids who immediately jumped into the water and began splashing each other. Meanwhile, Alan slathered suntan lotion all over his wife who reclined on a lounge with a big hat over her face. Alan was left to rub himself down after which he fell asleep on his lounge with a towel over his face and his hand across his mid-section.

Taylor, meanwhile, sat clothed at a table next to them under a huge umbrella sipping a latte. He watched the kids who had met some other kids who in turn were being watched by their parents. In spite of the din of the kids' screaming and constant chatter, he felt quite relaxed for someone who'd just escaped being murdered in his bed. But even that attack made things a bit clearer for him.

This wasn't about Alan or his family. Taylor now knew to a certainty that *he* was the target of a hit for some reason he couldn't yet guess. All he knew was that it apparently had to do with the fact that he'd made contact with Brooke Cameron, Bob Ross, and finally Tabby Young. Yet they never gave him anything, never imparted any information or secrets to him—not that he knew, anyway. He shook his head in dismay. That being the case, the only one who might have some idea as to what was going on would have to be the partner—Martin Millner. Hopefully Marge or Mott could get a line on this guy—preferably before the assassin got lucky. Meanwhile, Taylor now had yet another problem on his hands: he had to keep Alan and everyone else in the family from being injured by an assailant who was trying to get him.

"You are very thoughtful today, Mr. Taylor," someone said, interrupting his train of thought.

Taylor looked over to see the amiable Mr. Ulrich Kaiser nearing his table. He smiled.

"Take a seat," it's nice to sit by the water just watching the kids play."

Kaiser coughed as he took a seat and hooked his cane over the back of a neighboring chair. "In my day," he reported with a laugh, they had us in those youth camps, but we didn't have swimming pools; we swam in the sea."

"Yeah, I've read about the camps. What were they like—full-on indoctrination?"

Kaiser wagged his head. "Yes, there was a good deal of that, but basically it was more like being in the boy scouts, but with girls."

"Don't say?"

"Indeed. I was only there for a year or so, but it was wild. Everybody went swimming together—without bathing suits!"

"Yeah, I heard that too. What happened if the girls got pregnant?"

"Nobody cared, except maybe the parents, and they didn't count. The resulting babies became the wards of the Fatherland. Crazy bastards," he said as he shook his head with disgust.

"And apparently you didn't believe in that stuff."

"Not even a little. You see, I could sense the evil beneath it. They separated children from their parents for a political reason—in order to destroy the family unit. The same thing they're doing today in schools in America. I've seen it before, and it's the same old socialist crap. But the Marxists teachers' unions have invented even newer crap that's worse."

"Not everyone sees it that way today or did back in the day."

"Well, back then I certainly did, and I got away from it just as soon as I could and joined the Kriegsmarine."

"And that's where you left our story."

"Ja, ja. That's where I left my story," Kaiser repeated. "Understand, what I'm going to tell you was top, top secret at the time, never to be repeated to anyone."

"But you're telling me."

Kaiser waved a dismissive hand at Taylor. "They can't do anything to me now; I'm too old."

"And just why are you telling *me*?"

Kaiser wagged his head from side to side. "Because I sense in you a man of great discretion; a man who's seen a lot of things happen in the world but can keep it all to himself."

Taylor smiled a little. "Go ahead; tell your tale," he prompted the old man.

"But first something to drink," Kaiser insisted. He waved over the waiter and ordered an espresso. Then he took a great breath, and then he began.

"It was in the fall and winter of '38," he said. I was fortunate to have been picked for duty by the captain of the *Schwabenland*, Captain Ritscher. He hated the Nazis and picked men who were of a like mind like me. Anyway, the mission was completely secret, and we weren't told anything until after we'd already set sail. Later we found that the initial story they told us was complete baloney."

"What story was that?"

"Ach, ja. The High Command officially announced that we were going whaling because we needed to find more resources for fats for our population; you know, for butter, milk, cream, lard, cheese, bacon, margarine, salad oils, detergents, candles, linoleum and paints and such. But that's not really why we were on this trip at all."

At that point the waiter showed up with Kaiser's espresso to which the old man added a couple of heaping spoonfuls of sugar and then sipped at it.

"Aah, now where was I? Oh, yes," he reminded himself. "So, we left Bremenhafen and we're on the high seas on this supposed whaling ship about a week or so. The thing that was immediately suspicious, however, was that we were carrying two airplanes—two Donier Do JII flying boats. Why the hell do you need airplanes for whaling? When we saw those and then found out that there were over eighty, *eighty* research scientists on board mind you, we knew this trip wasn't about whale oil."

Kaiser took another sip and cleared his throat.

"After some time heading south, we eventually found ourselves at the northern end of Antarctica where we harbored."

"Yeeessss, I heard something about that a long time ago, but never the full story," Taylor interjected.

"Well, let me tell you, even so, you *never* would have heard the whole story. They wouldn't ever let it out."

Taylor sat back and sipped at his latte. "Okay, shoot," he returned skeptically. "What was the big secret?"

"I realize that you'll probably have a hard time believing this, but you must understand that we went there because two years before that there was a crash in the Black Forest near Freiburg."

Taylor rolled his eyes. "Oh, no. You're not talking about that fairytale flying saucer crash back in '36, are you?"

Kaiser sat more erect and frowned. "That is precisely what I am talking about," he stated, "and believe me, it was no fairytale."

"Really," retorted Taylor in a slightly dismissive tone. "How do you know that?"

"Because when the scientists needed an assistant, they chose me, and I eventually learned everything from them. Well, almost everything. They even showed me pictures."

"Pictures? Hm," grunted Taylor, relenting a bit. "All right. Go on."

"You see, somehow while they were reverse engineering the technology that they got from the crash, they found that there was some sort of connection to Antarctica, and that's why we had made the trip. And to allay your doubts that this was just some fluke, by the time we reached our destination, we were not just *one* ship but a flotilla of more than nine or ten ships including two submarines. The High Command would never have okayed such an expedition for a mere fairytale let alone for whale oil. And now the hunt was on."

Taylor rubbed his mouth thoughtfully. "And just *what* were you looking for?"

"We enlisted men weren't told, but since I had gained the confidence of the scientists, they confided in me and made me their cameraman. So they put me on one of their planes, gave me a camera and a bunch of film, and off we went."

Kaiser gulped down the rest of his espresso. Then he waved the waiter over and ordered another.

Taylor looked out across the pool as he had momentarily forgotten about the kids, but they seemed to be having fun. Someone had put a rubber raft in the pool, and all the kids were playing with it. Meanwhile, Cassandra Wells had turned over to tan her back while Alan was asleep and snoring, roasting his front side.

"So, does this begin to interest you?" Kaiser asked suddenly.

"Yes. Please go on with your story," said Taylor.

"Well, we covered a lot of territory that first day, about 600 square miles. I didn't know exactly what the scientists were looking for but they told me I'd know it when I saw it."

"And did you... see it, that is?"

The waiter brought over Kaiser's espresso and set it in front of him. Kaiser immediately added his sugar.

"See it... see it?" he mumbled and then looked straight at Taylor. "Yes. In fact, I was the very *first* to see it."

"And?" urged Taylor with a slightly exasperated edge to his voice.

"It was a huge gaping hole."

"That's it?" retorted Taylor. "A hole?"

"No, no. Wait. You don't understand. It was one of three or four such holes that we found. At first we thought they were caves. But on closer inspection, it turned out that they weren't just holes—they were massive. Maybe three-hundred yards or so in diameter."

"Natural sink holes, no doubt."

"That's what we thought in the first couple of days after we discovered them. But then one of the pilots decided to enter one of them."

"And what did you find?"

Kaiser took a large sip of his drink as he looked off in the horizon as though visualizing his experience once again.

"We flew into one of the holes without any trouble at all, and I can tell you; it was incredible. Like a gigantic bubble, a cavern hundreds of miles in every direction. A complete world under the ice. More than that, it was a green world with trees and lakes. The ambient temperature was seventy-three degrees."

"What!" returned Taylor incredulously.

"No, it's true. It's all true. We flew inside for a long time and then left. I took as many pictures as I could. We did not spot any fauna, but what we saw was enough. We flew back to the ship where we landed on the water next to it, and they rushed off my films to develop. They also swore me to secrecy. After that we who were in the plane were gathered to tell the rest of the scientists everything we could remember."

"Is that it?" asked Taylor.

"Most assuredly not. You see, after we told them what we had found, they set up the other plane for the next day."

Kaiser took another long draw off his espresso.

"And they, of course, found wondrous things?" put in Taylor.

Kaiser shook his head in the negative. "We who'd first discovered the cavern sat with the other scientists as the plane went to reconnoiter where we had been. We could hear them on the wireless. When they first went in, everything seemed fine. Then suddenly the wireless went static for a few moments. And then all we heard was 'Mayday, Mayday, Mayday!'"

Taylor frowned. "What happened?"

"The plane was being chased by a number of... well they were flying saucers."

"Come on!" Taylor shot back.

"No, it is true. I saw them with my own eyes," he insisted animatedly as he pointed at his eyes. "Five of them followed the plane back to the ship. They were gleaming silver metal, large, the size of a soccer field. And then..."

"Then what?"

"The plane was vaporized in midair by a ray it as soon as it came in range. Poof! Just like that. Then the saucers fired on some of the other ships which caught fire, exploded and sank. And when we turned our guns on them, they sent a ray at us that froze the weapons so they couldn't fire. Later we found that their mechanical parts had been melted together as though a welder had fused them."

"Was that the end of it then?"

"Almost. Their ships formed a semicircle in the sky around our fleet and just hovered a hundred feet up in the sky without moving."

"For how long?"

"Seemed like an eternity. Finally, Captain Ritscher weighed anchor as did the remaining ships, and we all got the hell out of there as quickly as we could."

"And that was it?"

"Not quite. As we were leaving, I looked back with some binoculars and saw a gigantic craft, a mother ship, approach the others from above. All the smaller ships disappeared into that ship, and that huge ship zoomed straight up at an unbelievable speed and disappeared in space."

Kaiser stopped. He took a couple of breaths as though he'd been running and sipped more of his espresso.

Taylor drummed his fingers on the table. Then he finished off his latte. "Interesting story, but I've heard other stories that rival yours about Area 51, Roswell, yadda, yadda, yadda. Forgive me for being skeptical. I also don't believe in the tooth fairy."

Kaiser snorted a laugh. "I don't mind your skepticism at all, Mr. Taylor. But, you know, you can never tell when things you believe are fiction turn out to be fact. That experience—which I witnessed *with my own eyes*—changed my life completely and changed the direction of my life from that point on."

Kaiser stood up from his chair and grabbed his cane.

"Anyway, I just thought you might find my story interesting if not illuminating," he added with a smile.

"Thank you. It was... uh, very entertaining if not also illuminating."

Kaiser began to walk off. "That is all I intended. But you might share the story with your friend Beatrice Jolly; that is, if you get the chance. Good day, sir," said Kaiser as he sauntered off into the afternoon sun as the kids in the pool continued to laugh and scream their delight at being young.

"Beatrice Jolly? What?" repeated Taylor. "How the hell..." he was just saying to himself when his phone went off.

It was Mott.

"Theo," he answered. "What's up?"

"About your friend Robert Ross..."

"Yeah?"

"The airline turned his body over to the authorities in Barcelona where you landed. They did an autopsy."

"And found what?" asked Taylor.

"He was murdered, Taylor. Poisoned."

CHAPTER 6

"Taylor. Taylor," he suddenly heard as little Curtis and Amy came running up to him dripping wet. "Can you take us to see cartoons at the Magic Theater?" they asked.

Taylor reached over, grabbed a couple of towels, and gave one to each kid.

"Dry off. Sure we can go. We just have to tell your mom and dad," he said.

At the mention of the parents, Curtis ran over to his father and shook him awake.

"Daddy, wake up. Can Taylor take us to the Magic Theater to see cartoons?"

Alan Wells woke from his sleep with a start and in pain, for he'd gotten sunburned rather graphically all over the front of his body.

"Ah, ah... Oh, my God. I'm burnt," he said which awakened Cassandra. She gave him a fish eye.

"Didn't you use the sunblock like I told you?"

"Yeah, yeah," he replied, "but I fell asleep. Oh, my God, look at my stomach!"

Taylor had to suppress a laugh, for Alan had fallen asleep with his hand over his stomach and now sported a perfect blank of his hand and arm on his mid-section. His face was also pale since he had put a towel over it. However, the rest of his chest was the hue of a Maine lobster.

"Better get some aloe on that," Taylor suggested.

"Aw, man this hurts," complained Alan. Then he looked at the kids. "I have to go upstairs and take care of this," he said to them. "I don't know if..."

"But we can go, can't we?" pressed Amy.

"Tell you what," interrupted Taylor. "We'll all go upstairs. Mom and Dad can take care of themselves, and you two kids can get out of your wet suits and into some dry clothes. I'll take you to the theater if that's all right with your parents."

"Well, thank you very much, Taylor," replied Cassandra with surprising grace. "The sun has worn me out. I'm all greasy. I think I'd like a nice long bath. Alan can lick his wounds and rest up till dinner. Thank you," she repeated once again. "Mandy can help when she gets back."

The kids hollered and wrapped their towels about themselves. Then the whole group got up and headed for their staterooms.

Cartoons aren't what they used to be, decided Taylor after sitting in the dark for a half-hour watching some of the Magic Theater's offerings. The main problem—even if you liked cartoons—was that the old cartoons actually were made by adults with a sense of adult humor and sometimes even great wit behind them. The new ones, on the other hand, it seemed to him were made for imbeciles. No wonder the country's going down the tubes, he thought.

"Hi!" he heard suddenly as someone sat down next to him. It was Mandy.

"Whoa, you're back. Did you and the girls have fun?"

"Oh, yes. Lots. We just laughed and laughed and enjoyed everything we saw. But even fun can be tiring."

He chuckled beneath the noise of the film. "I hear you," he said, "but you needn't have come down. You could have rested. This can't last long."

She checked out the screen. "Ah, this series."

"Huh?" he said.

"You've got about forty-five minutes to go. They've got three different series of cartoons. I've see 'em all a bunch of times. This one will be done in about forty-five minutes."

"That's good because I think I'll go batty and need a drool cup if it continues much longer than that."

She nodded. "But the kids love it. I don't get it, but they can watch the same thing time after time after time."

He grunted. "The kids deserve better stuff."

"Yeah probably, but it's all they've got now."

Taylor shook his head. "Ya wanna get a cup of coffee?" he asked. "There's a coffee bar just outside."

She thought a second. "Sure," she replied, "I guess we can leave them in here if we're not too far away, but just let me tell them where we'll be," she said and then bent over and whispered to Amy and Curtis.

They left the theater and walked the few steps to the bar when someone walked into them.

"Mandy!" exclaimed the girl with the sandy-colored hair and big smile.

"Oh, Casey. Hi. We're just going to get some coffee. Want to join us? she asked.

"Is this him?" asked Casey.

"Uh, yes. Taylor, this is my friend Casey—Casey Stone. She toured Rome with me today."

Taylor shook her hand. "Pleased to meet you. You had a good time in the city?"

"It was so terrific!" replied the young lady, bursting with enthusiasm. "And thank you so much or letting us use the limousine. I felt like royalty," she gushed with that big smile on her face.

"Well, it wasn't my doing. But... say, wouldn't you really like to have some coffee with us?"

"Oh, no, no. Thanks but I'll be going. Anyway, three's a crowd," she said. Then she waved at Mandy. "Have a good time. And see you at the pool," she added with a little wink and was off.

"Hm," grunted Taylor. "Seems like a nice girl."

"She *is*," returned Mandy. "And she's a lot of fun."

"Speaking of fun. Did you also have good time this afternoon?" asked Mandy slightly sarcastically once they'd gotten their drinks at the coffee bar and sat down.

He grinned. "And you do this every day!" he declared incredulously.

"Naw, it's not so bad, especially if they're good kids—and these are really good kids."

He laughed. "Okay. Whatever you say. "So..." he began, changing the topic, "so what did you do in Rome?"

From that point on, it was a lengthy monologue as Taylor suspected it would be. Mandy went on about how nice it was that Wells had let her and her friends, Anna and Casey travel in the limo to see the sights. Then she related the details of the trip, the places they went—the Vatican with Michelangelo's *pietà*, the Spanish Steps, the Baths of Caracalla, the Colosseum, the Piazza Navona, yadda, yadda, yadda—the things they saw, the things they bought, the food they ate, and the prices they paid for everything. He was wiped out just listening to her. At some point in the narrative, Taylor saw Palfrey across the way waving for him to join him.

"As nice as this has been," he said finally to Mandy who looked up a little surprised, "I'm going to have to get back to my room to make some calls. See you at dinner? Oh... can you take care of the kids?"

"Uh... yes," she replied caught off guard. "All right. I guess I'll go back in and join them. At least it's dark in there and cool. I may be able to snooze."

Taylor chuckled and gave her a little wave as he headed off in the other direction. As soon as he met Palfrey, the fellow was all business.

"Come with me," said Palfrey.

"Why? What'd you find out?" asked Taylor.

"Just follow me," repeated Palfrey as he walked quickly. "Your questions will be answered soon enough."

It took no time at all for the pair to reach the elevator which took them to Taylor's deck. But instead of taking the corridor in the direction of his stateroom, Palfrey led him out to the starboard, open-air side of the ship where the bulkhead for the individual verandas began. Captain Drake and Dr. Wyndham-Smythe stood looking at the decking around the area while two other sailors were on their knees involved in a close inspection with magnifying glasses, cameras, and a tape measure.

"Ah, there you are," said Drake.

"What's up, Captain?" asked Taylor.

"Well, it seems that the chap that attacked you came round this way," Wyndham-Smythe began...

"And he left footprints here," stated the captain who then turned to his men. "Do you have it there, Smithers?"

A solidly-built young man stood up. "Yes, sir," replied the sailor. "I took several close ups of the tracks with the infrared camera both here and on the veranda. I'll run them up on the computer, and we'll have a better idea of what we've got and who we're dealing with. Ian will get copies with the acetate strips, and when we have those two things together, we should have a cracking piece of evidence, sir."

"Excellent!" returned Drake. "Get back to me the moment you two have anything."

"Easy peasy, sir," replied Smithers. It should only take us maybe an hour or so to get something preliminary." Then he turned to his compatriot. "C'mon, Ian," he said. "Let's get this kit to the lab," and off they went.

"Yes," interrupted Wyndham-Smythe, "it appears the fellow made it around each of the bulwarks to your veranda and escaped the same way. However, when he got to this point, he must have jumped because he left a print of at least one of his shoes and other traces that an infrared camera can pick up. Our chaps say the pictures they take and computerize can give us real detail and a lot of other information. Give them enough time, and they can give you his phone number."

Taylor chuckled. "Not even our forensics lab back home can do that," he returned.

"And there's more. We were able to examine the knife closely," Palfrey began.

"What about it?"

"Interesting blade," he reported. "It's made of German steel. The handle is made of African Panga Panga wood which is about as strong as steel. The pommel and guard are made of polished brass. The whole thing's a fairly expensive piece of kit. Probably cost a few hundred quid. Maybe more. My guess is that it's something a professional would likely use."

"Umm. Made where?"

"Difficult to say," replied Palfrey as he squinted into the distance. "Italy, possibly. Maybe Pakistan. But that's not the best thing about the knife."

"What is?" asked Taylor.

Palfrey smiled cagily. "Under close examination we found a partial fingerprint on the blade just near the guard."

Taylor smiled. "No."

"Yes!" Palfrey shot back, but unfortunately it's not enough to identify anyone. "But then we also found..."

"What?"

"A small trace of blood where the blade meets the guard. We checked that out too, and it was Tabitha Young's blood. This was the weapon used to kill her."

"Whoa! Well done! I certainly have to give it to you folks. Outstanding."

Captain Drake rocked back and forth on his heels a little. "Well, we do fairly well, Mr. Taylor. We do fairly well."

That was an understatement.

The group repaired to the captain's ready room and waited for Smithers and Ian to return which, indeed took something over an hour. But when they returned, they brought some great information with them, and Smithers made the report.

"From where the fellow jumped to the deck and then loped off down the walkway, from the length of his gait we put his height at about five-foot-ten. He must weigh about one-sixty. Thin build, and from the pressure we see where his stance is more solid, he's a righty. The smudges on the knife handle also indicated that—right handed."

"What about the shoes?" inquired Wyndham-Smythe. "Anything on their brand?"

"They're an American brand deck shoe. We checked the tread marks on the bottom with our database. They're Vans; nearly new ones. You can tell by the detailed imprint of the tread. We didn't get anything off of the rug in your stateroom, but we found similar patterned shoe marks on your veranda as also on the two other verandas that led from your neighbor's to the exterior bulkhead. He wore rubber gloves the whole time, so there weren't any fingerprints just smudges. However, where he held on to two of the separators between two of the verandas, he definitely left traces of the size and shape of his hand. Thus we found three squarish handprints and—from the strength required to negotiate the path to your veranda—we guess that this guy's pretty strong."

"So... do you also have his phone number?" asked Taylor blankly.

All of the others laughed aloud.

"Not quite yet," replied the captain. "But seriously, he's tried to get to you at least once under difficult circumstances, do you wish to continue to place yourself in jeopardy?"

"As they like to say in South Texas, this ain't my first rodeo, Captain Drake. I think I can handle myself pretty well when it gets right down to it."

"And the family you're watching over?"

"As long as I'm watching the mister and his wife, I have to be on the same alert as though I were watching out for myself."

"Understand," replied the captain. "But would you mind if we kept an eye on you and your group... from afar? We won't interfere with anything unless there's a serious attack."

"That would be fine," replied Taylor. "Please watch their nanny, Miss Bannon, and especially the kids, Curtis and Amy. I wouldn't want anything to happen to any of them."

The captain stood up and looked at the other five individuals around him. "Then, gentlemen, I suppose we're done here," he said.

———

The next morning the ship was anchored at Naples which looked more like a modern port and not an industrial complex. As usual, while the other passengers were waiting to catch bus rides and private tours with the Ishia busses, Alan had his limo waiting to whisk everyone off to see the sights, and today those sights included the ancient city of Pompeii and then the town of Naples itself.

Cassandra had never seen Pompeii and was eager to visit the ancient Roman settlement. Moreover, she wanted everyone to come along—especially the children—since it would be a cultural excursion not to be missed. So they loaded everyone into the limo and headed off to see the once buried city.

Above the entrance loomed the words Scavi Di Pompei, whatever that meant. After that it was a matter of hiking all over the place by foot which gave Taylor the chance to check out the footwear others were sporting. In fact, the only

Vans sneakers he saw on this trip were worn by teenage girls. At length, he stopped checking out people's shoes and viewed the city—such as it was.

It was a wonder how people must have lived back in 79 AD when Vesuvius blew and entombed the city in a thirty-foot-deep sepulcher of ash. Pompeii seemed a warren of little stone-paved lanes with the remains of small businesses and houses on either side of the allées. The villas had roofs that looked almost exactly like modern Spanish tiles. The insides of the places had garish paintings, some of daily life and others with plenty of sex imagery worthy of a porno magazine. Whenever the group rounded a corner and ran into one of these, Cassandra quickly steered the children in the opposite direction.

More interesting was the little suburb of Herculaneum. It was where the general populace lived. You could still see the shops and even goods like bread laid out just as it was the day the town was destroyed. Laid out too were the bodies of the deceased encased in hardened ash who didn't get a chance to escape the volcanic eruption. Cassandra also steered the kids away from viewing those although Curtis kept running back to look at them. After a couple of hours, they'd had all they needed of Pompeii.

After that it was a trip into Naples itself. The driver and guide suggested that they experience urban Italy by walking through the Sanitá district of Naples where tourists meandered through the streets shoulder to shoulder which drove Taylor nuts trying to keep an eagle eye on Alan—but he managed it. The group grabbed pizza for lunch and stood around a tall table sharing Napoli's hometown fare.

Alan had wanted to visit a place that he said he heard about in a travelogue called the Fontanelle Ossuary where the remains of the previous inhabitants of the local church's cemeteries now resided on full display, but Cassandra quickly nixed the idea lest she and the kids would get grossed out and scared. She preferred things of beauty and couldn't understand why Alan couldn't have paid the captain to make the ship stop at Capri which was what she really had wanted to see. Her girlfriend Joy told her it was a spot that shouldn't be missed because of its Blue Grotto. Alan countered that they'd do it on their next trip. Just not today.

The group had been gone for several hours, Alan's sunburn was driving him crazy, and by now everyone was getting tired. The kids were getting cranky. Time to return to the ship. As usual, the limo dropped them off at the dock where everybody piled out. Alan left a generous tip for the driver even over the considerable amount of cash that the guy already was getting paid. He didn't have to do that, of course—but that was Alan.

Once on board, the group dragged themselves to their respective staterooms to freshen up and maybe take a little nap before dinner. Taylor, on the other hand, had to get updated on the cases with which he was dealing—Tabitha Young's and his own.

Marge had sent him a folder full of information on his phone which he sat and perused. It seemed that the business run by Bob Ross and Martin Millner was a small part of a tangle of businesses that seemed at its core might be owned by some large conglomerate—or not. Marge was still working on that one. Anyway, she wrote that their business indeed dealt in antiques and in selling stuff on consignment—expensive stuff—on the order of several million dollars kind of stuff. Still, she had no idea what he was presently dealing with or where Martin Millner was currently located. He'd disappeared.

"Terrific!" groused Taylor.

Beyond that, Marge reported that she was still turning over stones and would contact him again if she came up with anything new. Taylor wrote back that she'd done an exceptional job finding this material. She wrote back that if it was that good, then great, he could get her a raise to which he said he'd try.

After closing out that folder, he opened up another from Mott. It repeated the fact that Bob Ross died from poisoning, and then it traced his background—stuff that Marge couldn't get. It seemed that the young man lived on the edge of legality having been charged with civil actions a couple of time but escaped any legal liability. Apparently, Ross and Millner were friends from their youth in North Carolina where Ross knew Tabitha from their days in high school.

And Millner? His past was really murky, but again as Marge had pointed out, he was just gone—disappeared, and no one knew when, where, or how.

Taylor's head hurt. He chalked it up to a bit of sunstroke that he probably got sitting next to the pool where the sun reflected on him. He grabbed a couple Bayer aspirin from a bottle in his bag and tossed them down with a swig from a water bottle. He twisted the cap back on the bottle and stared at the wall for a second. He needed a latte.

He sat at the same bar where he'd first met Ulrich Kaiser a couple of days ago, but the old guy wasn't there today. He smirked to himself about the old man's wild-ass story and particularly that he mentioned Beatrice Jolly? Jesus, how the hell did he know her, and more important, how the hell did he know that Taylor knew her? One thing was for sure, the two of them really went for those UFO conspiracy stories—or what they currently called UAP conspiracy stories since the navy released video of actual vehicles that looked like Tic Tacs. Whatever they were, Taylor couldn't figure out whose conspiracy story was wilder, Kaiser's or Bea's. He nodded to himself that he'd have to write her about this new wrinkle in his biography.

As he sipped at his latte, he suddenly became aware that someone was staring at him.

"Mr. Taylor?" said the man.

Taylor look over to see the affable fellow he met at the coffee bar the same day he met Kaiser.

"Oh, yes. Ari?" he responded.

The fellow laughed. "Ardie. Close enough," he returned.

"No it's not, and I apologize," replied Taylor briskly. "You got *my* name right, and I didn't get *yours* right. Let me treat you to a coffee," he said.

"No, no," protested Ardie.

"What's the difference?" Taylor shot back. "Don't forget, we don't pay for them anyway. Only for alcoholic drinks."

Both men laughed. "Mike!" said Taylor, "a... um... an Arabica with warm cream for my friend here," he ordered. "Right?"

"Comin' right up, mate," replied Mike who instantly got to work.

"Well, you certainly didn't forget my drink!" exclaimed Ardie.

"Probably because I pay closer attention to coffee than to people," he chuckled. "Anyway, how's the cruise coming along?" he asked as the barkeep produced the beverage.

It was then that he involuntarily looked at the man's shoes—something he'd been doing all day in Naples since he was on the hunt for anyone wearing Vans. Ardie's shoes were brown suede loafers and looked like Bruno Maglis. He remembered that his buddy Maat Rokkah back home had a pair of these. They always made him wonder. Who the hell needed to pay three-hundred bucks for a pair of shoes?

"Something wrong with my shoes? Did I step in something?" Ardi asked as he looked around on the deck as he sipped his drink.

Taylor caught himself and chuckled. "No, no. I'm sorry, I just remembered that a friend of mine also has a pair of those. I wondered what the attraction was?"

"Comfort, of course," Ardie replied. "Like my father always said, there's nothing better than a good, comfortable pair of shoes. He was right. I'll pay anything for that."

"And apparently so will my friend," returned Taylor with a chuckle. "But as I was saying, how are you enjoying the cruise?"

"Well, my wife is certainly enjoying the pool and the beauty lounge—getting a massage, her hair done, her nails manicured—I can assure you of that. But as far as I'm concerned, if I have to watch just one more animated princess movie, I think I'll jump off the ship."

Taylor snorted a laugh and had to work to not dribble the sip of coffee he just took. "I hear ya," he agreed. "But I guess that's what this place is mostly set up for—kids."

Ardie nodded and took a final tug off his coffee. "Yeah, I guess," he returned with a resigned tone. "You have any kids?" he asked.

"Naw. My cousin does, and I've watched over them, so I know what you're talking about."

Ardie raised his left wrist to check his watch. "Yes, well, I'm due back on dad duty and then have to get us ready for... where are we tomorrow?"

"Malta."

"Ah, yes, Malta," he repeated as he finished off his brew. "Well, have fun. See you around. Maybe in Malta," he added. Taylor nodded, and Ardie then walked off.

In the morning, the ship anchored in the harbor at Malta, the island country that stood behind monumental sandstone-colored ramparts plunk in the middle of the Mediterranean Sea. It had not changed so much since Napoleon had done the same thing in 1798 on his way to Egypt when he fought the rusty old Knights of Malta. But in his case, his military force beat them to a pulp and then made off with all the wealth they possessed including twelve life-sized solid silver statues of Christ's Disciples which were never to be seen again. Yet another one of those little mysteries in history.

The previous evening after the trying day in Naples did not end well for the group. Everyone was so tired—including the kids—that no one at the dinner table said more than five words the whole time. They ate; they headed for bed.

Taylor was so fried that he flopped on the bed and went out like a light without getting out of his clothes. As a result, he woke up feeling raw in the morning. He took a hot shower and just let the hot water wash over his face to wake him up. That seemed to do the trick.

Once he was dressed he checked his phone, and once again there were no messages from Marge or Mott. The ship's crew hadn't contacted him either. Time for breakfast. He always ate earlier than the family which freed him up to keep tabs more effectively on Alan and his environment.

As he usually did each morning, Taylor went directly to the breakfast buffet where he grabbed a plate and piled on scrambled eggs, hash browns, a half-dozen sausages, a couple of biscuits, and a latte. Along the way he picked up a couple of packets of butter and blackberry jam. Then he looked for a table where he could eat in peace. But it was not to be.

"I say there, old man," came that by now familiar British inflection, "mind if I finish my cuppa while you dine?" inquired Dr. Wyndham-Smythe pointing at his Styrofoam cup of tea.

Taylor nodded and started in on his repast. "Sure," he managed to get out, mouth half full.

Wyndham-Smythe took the chair to his right side. "I just wanted to tell you that we haven't found anything else yet," he imparted breathlessly.

Taylor grunted and nodded.

"Yes, of course I was wondering if you thought that. But believe me, we've been on this thing every second since it happened."

Taylor nodded again.

"And I agree with you completely," he went on. "There could be trouble in Malta once we get there. Valletta is a great city, but I'd suggest you watch out particularly on those little choked lanes. All sorts of devilment could occur there— a real hugger-mugger if you take my meaning."

Taylor nodded as intelligently as he could.

"Indeed, I was sure you'd think the same thing about those criminal types," returned Wyndham-Smythe. "You can never tell what those johnnies will be up to. Well, I should be off," he said at last as he sipped the last drops from his cup. "Great to have had this little talk. It's good to have everything clear."

Taylor nodded again.

"Yes, I agree. But just rest assured that we're on the case. Ciao!" said Dr. Wyndham-Smythe who waved and was finally and blissfully off, leaving Taylor the solitude he required to plan for the day.

As usual, the limo would be waiting for the family, and today Cassandra wanted everyone to see the sights. She figured that since Britain had controlled Malta up until the middle of the last century that there was no language barrier like they had experienced in France and Italy.

She had already made out a list of places she wished to see on the recommendation of her girlfriends back in L.A.

who had toured the island last year. Alan couldn't stand any of them, but whatever Cassandra wanted, she got. And so they had to hit the places that the girls talked about so animatedly during their hen parties. There was no way out of it.

First there were the shops with beautiful blown glass. Cassandra's girlfriend Kaitlin, the stockbroker's wife, had gotten a gorgeous vase in one particular shop. Thus, the whole group stopped there, and Cassandra made a purchase with Alan's credit card. Then, of course, there were the shops that dealt with filigree jewelry that Carol, the attorney's wife, had mentioned. Lastly, there were the shops that dealt in fine lace that Brittney, the basketball player's wife, had told her about. More purchases. The guys and the kids couldn't see this stuff for dust, of course, but Cassandra and Mandy had a grand time. Surprisingly, at one point Taylor saw Ardie walk out of a neighboring shop apparently with a woman who was holding a little girl. He wasn't sure if Ardie was really with them or if he had even seen him, but when Taylor saw him walk by, his smile dropped precipitously. For as he looked at his feet, he couldn't help but notice that the man was wearing tennis shoes—Vans.

The last place they shopped at was a shop that sold prickly pear jam. Cassandra's friend Joy—who Alan called an obnoxious, fat know-it-all who was anything but joyous—had brought some back from Malta last year, and all the girls found it beyond delicious. Cassandra bought a case.

As the group made their way through these places, Cassandra would purchase other little tchotchkes. Alfonse, the driver, would put the purchases in the car trunk, and then they'd move on to the next venue. In the end, Alfonse would have everything wrapped and sent to Alan's home address in Brentwood. There was no need for the fam to schlepp stuff around with them.

Aside from seeing the cityscape, they also took the half-day prehistoric Ghar Dalam Cave and Megalithic Temple tour. By the time they finished shopping, the tour busses from the ship had caught up with them. But because they'd purchased tickets in advance of the trip, they didn't have to stand in line with the rest of the schlubs from the ship who didn't have the brains to plan ahead. Mandy waved at a couple of the women standing in line whom she knew from the pool as the fam walked by into the place.

The museum was chock full of the extinct animals that used to inhabit Malta going back to the ice age: dwarf elephants, hippopotami, giant swans, ancient bears, deer, and other such fauna. The kids seemed to like seeing this stuff. Mandy asked Taylor if he'd carry her back pack so that she could bend down to explain things to the kids better. Of course, he acquiesced and slipped it over his right shoulder.

But the real treat were the prehistoric caves. They dated back to the ice age that meandered underground with dramatic lighting, where everything echoed in the dingy light. The kids were a little scared and clung onto Mandy and their father who led the group while Taylor hung to the rear ahead of the crush of ship tourists to be in a good position to protect Alan against anything coming from that quarter. They all followed a docent who kept up a well-practiced running narrative of the history of the caves.

Suddenly, when they were well into the cave, the light blipped out. All the kids screamed and some of the adults gasped. The docent shouted to everyone to stay where they were while he spoke to someone else. This happened occasionally; nothing to fear. As Taylor stood squinting into the darkness, he was suddenly bumped by someone. He reflexively jerked to the right just as the person mumbled "sorry" and moved away. In less than a minute the lights came back on. The docent apologized and everyone moved forward. Taylor checked Alan and the rest of the fam who were all in place and in good shape. The crowd pushed on like bovines on their way to the slaughter house until they finally emerged from the cave into the daylight which caused everyone to squint until their eyesight had adjusted.

The crowd started to break up to head for the busses. Mandy left the kids to walk over to Taylor.

"I'll take that," she said as she went to take her backpack off his shoulder.

Taylor smiled and started to slip off the backpack but stopped short suddenly.

"Uh, let me keep it," he said. "It's not that much of a bother. After all, the kids need you more than you need the backpack. I'll give it to you when we get to the car."

"If you insist," replied Mandy with a smile and returned to her charges.

"I insist," he replied with a grin.

Then he turned to Alan and told him he needed to use the restroom. Alan and the family should stay exactly where they were and not move until he returned. It was so unusual a request that Alan agreed immediately. Taylor smiled and walked off.

He moved quickly to the restroom which fortunately had mostly emptied itself. He went directly to the broad, marble wash counter and carefully set the backpack down. He turned it over to reveal something that had gotten snagged on one of the shoulder straps. It was some sort of bulb connected to a syringe. It couldn't have held more than a few units of liquid and was probably easier to use than those orange cap-colored syringes that drug attics regularly left lying all over the streets, sidewalks, and park grounds of San Francisco. With this thing, all you had to do was stick it in and squeeze the little bulb. He carefully detached it from the strap and bent the quarter-inch needle harmlessly backwards. Then he wrapped it in several layers of paper towels and put it into his coat pocket. He checked over the backpack which he had to open to remove whatever the needle had pierced. Curiously, the needle had gone right into an apple; he could see the mark it left. There was also a sandwich that was wrapped. He carefully took both items out of the bag and dumped them into the sink where he turned the water on and jabbed them with his keys until they turned into a mushy mass. When he was satisfied that it was free of whatever was in the syringe, he picked the stuff up with a paper towel and dumped the remains into the trash. He then emptied out everything else in the bag and rinsed the affected part with soap and water. He dried it as best he could with paper towels. Finally, he checked everything he'd dumped out to make sure that whatever was in the syringe didn't contaminate Mandy's goods. Being satisfied, he put everything back in, slipped the backpack over his shoulder, left the restroom, and returned to the family.

"You took so long that I thought we were going to have to rent an apartment," Alan put in jocularly.

"Sorry. Something didn't agree with me," he explained.

Mandy walked up and snatched her backpack off his arm. "Thanks, I'll take that now," she said. However, when she was going to put it on, she stopped. "Hey, this thing's all damp," she groused.

"Uh, sorry for that," returned Taylor sheepishly. "When I put it on the counter, it slipped into the sink and everything fell out. Some stuff accidentally got all wet. The apple and your sandwich fell on the floor, and I thought it best to just dump them. I'll get you replacements later, I promise."

Mandy frowned. "And I put that sandwich together myself."

"Don't worry, Mandy," Alan put in jocularly. "If he doesn't come through for you, Cass and I will."

Mandy smiled but then put the damp backpack back onto Taylor's shoulder. "Here," she said. "You can carry it until it dries."

Taylor laughed it off but took a big breath of relief that he had escaped what he was sure was the certain death contained in that syringe.

It was late in the day when the limo got back to the dock. One again the fam piled out of the limo, and Alan patted the driver on the shoulder and left him a sizable tip. The group tapped their ID cards on the reader and got on board. Everyone went to his stateroom to rest up before dinner. Everyone except for Taylor.

He buzzed Palfrey and then made his way to the bridge where his trio of contacts awaited him. He took the wadded up paper out of his jacket and handed it to Dr. Wyndham-Smythe.

"Be careful with that. I think it's poison."

"Poison?" repeated Captain Drake.

"Yeah. I was in the caves on a tour. Lights went out, someone bumped me, and I found this—a syringe."

"Good God!" exclaimed Palfrey.

"Luckily, I was holding a backpack when the fellow bumped me. I jerked to the side and apparently the syringe snagged on one of the bag's belts. Otherwise, the fellow would have taken it so as not to leave evidence."

"Any idea what was in it?" asked the doctor.

"I haven't the foggiest. Think you can figure that out?"

"I should say!" replied Wyndham-Smythe confidently.

"But there's something else," he said. "There's a fellow I met at a coffee bar named Ardie; that is, Ardeth Bey.

Please check this guy out. He wears Vans of the type we suspect the assailant wore."

"I'll get right on it, sir, and will get back to you as soon as I find something," replied Palfrey. With that, he rang off.

Taylor got out of his duds and took a long, hot shower while he ran over the permutations of what had happened during the day and what they might mean. Ardie looked a little spare for the guy who had attacked him. Then again, it was in the middle of the night, and he'd been awakened from a dead sleep.

Then he sat at the table in his room and checked his phone. There were messages from both Marge and Mott.

Marge reported that she found the incorporation papers for Ross' and Millner's Florida business that went back five years and was called Sunshine Collectibles LLC. The business principally dealt in high-end goods from valuable paintings to precious antiques to one-of-a-kind objects. They acted as go-betweens in bringing priceless objects to auction houses like Adolf Hitler's Parade Staff Car and Gary Cooper's 1935 Duesenberg that was one of two ever built. They were involved in obtaining a dinosaur skeleton that was auctioned for millions. Apparently, they made a pretty penny off of all of these deals. We're talking eventual sales in the neighborhood of the twenty and thirty millions of dollars. They had a part in the sale of a Rembrandt that finally auctioned for $193 million dollars and that crazy Banksy painting that shredded itself at auction and went for over $25 million. From all Marge could gather, they were currently working on yet another exotic deal like this, but she had no clue what it was. What she could say confidently was that they were backed by a big conglomerate that always stayed behind the scene. Anyway, that's all she got. "And what about that raise?" she added.

Taylor considered the information for a moment before he opened up Mott's e-mail. A couple of clicks, and there it was.

Mott reported that he had in fact been able to get some info on Ross and Millner. Apparently, Ross always stayed on the East Coast. Yeah, he was born and raised in North Carolina, but his moves were to South Carolina, New York, Massachusetts, Rhode Island, and then down to Florida where he started a business with Millner. During his travels he'd gotten in with some heavy hitters in the Hamptons, but we don't know what he was up to—just that he was there.

Martin Millner, who also grew up in North Carolina, had also worked in New York, New Jersey, and Rhode Island, but he also came to California. Mott had him in L.A. working for a company called Wanderlust Cruises and at another called Kavright Inc. It was apparently some sort of international trading company. Then, back about five years or so, Millner went to Florida and opened a business with Ross where he's been ever since. "And he's done well," Mott reported. "Owns a rather large spread in Jupiter, Florida. At present we think he may be in L.A., but we're not sure. We'll let you know if we find something," he concluded.

Taylor stared straight ahead, nodded, and folded his lip. Could this be the guy, he wondered. He quickly answered Mott's missive and asked for a picture of Millner and any other info he might have on him—including height, weight, and fingerprints, if any.

CHAPTER 7

As Taylor was absorbing this news, his phone text beeped. It was Alan. Everyone was set to go to dinner. Taylor messaged back that he'd be there in a sec. He tossed his phone on the bed and went to put on his dinner duds.

Dinner was tasty as always, and the family was more talkative than the previous day. Apparently, they were becoming used to the rigors of vacation travel. The kids wanted to go to a cartoon movie after dinner, and the parents passed them off to Mandy to do that. Alan and Cassandra, on the other hand wanted to go to the so-called Midnight Lounge where there were adult beverages and stand up. Kids weren't allowed since the humor was often raunchy and not fit for their tender ears. Taylor, of course, would accompany them even though he found most of this kind of humor hit and miss, and in the age of the woke, mostly miss.

The place was packed, and the heavy odor of alcohol permeated the joint. The room was set up like one of those clubs you'd find in L.A. or New York. Small tables that went back several rows from a small stage where the comic performed. Tonight the headliner was Roscoe T. Russell, a comic who apparently had successfully played in a number of big cities across the globe. His humor was not just raunchy but flat out filthy. The f-word was every other word, but the audience surprisingly seemed to accept it as regular speech. Taylor, who hadn't seen any stand up for a few years, began to think of himself as an old prude. He didn't mind humor that was edgy, but below-the-belt filthy banter never interested him. Unfortunately, the current comic's taste wasn't Taylor's which made for a long evening. Eventually, the couple decided to pack it in. They'd had their fill of alcohol and of Roscoe T. Russell's brand of hilarity. They didn't have to get up early the next day since it was a cruise day, and they wouldn't reach port until the day after that.

The parents checked in with Mandy before they hit the sack. The kids had had a great time. Tomorrow Curtis wanted to swim but Amy wanted her mother to take her to the princess fair where she could get all dolled up as a fantasy princess.

As for Taylor, he dragged himself into his cabin and dropped into a lounge chair. It had been long day. He checked his phone, but there were no messages. Suddenly, his phone rang, and he answered expectantly.

"Taylor," he responded at once.

"Yes," replied the speaker in breathy British speak. "Wyndham-Smythe here. I have the results of the analysis. Would you care to discuss them?"

"Not over the phone," Taylor replied. "Can you meet me at the coffee bar on deck 12?"

"Be there in a thrice," the doctor agreed.

Turns out, the "thrice" was a little longer than Taylor had expected, so he ordered a latte which he nursed until the good doctor appeared after about ten minutes. They took a table off to the side.

"So sorry, old man, but a fellow with a cut arm needed some attention. Apparently his wife threw a bottle at him in their cabin, and it broke and cut his arm. Horrible gash. Took fifteen stitches to seal up the thing," he explained.

"And you found?"

"Found? Found what?" the doctor replied blankly.

"The analysis," Taylor pressed.

"Oh, of course, of course," said Wyndham-Smythe as he fumbled with a folder he was carrying. "Here's the stuff," he said proudly as he laid it open in front of Taylor.

He took out a silver Cross pen and pointed to places on the first page as he explained the findings.

"As you can see," he began, "there was leakage from the syringe where the needle was bent. Good thinking, that!"

"Thanks."

"Now, even if we didn't have that evidence, there was also a little more liquid left in the bulb portion of the syringe itself as you can see here," he continued as he tapped on a blown-up picture of the syringe.

"We didn't find any fingerprints or even partials on the rubber bulb or on the plastic parts. Everything was clean. So, we were mostly left with the liquid alone. You were, of course, wise to avoid touching it. You never can tell how toxic or caustic something like that might be."

"Right. So? What was it?"

"Tetrodotoxin," he answered straight away. "It's found in puffer fish and in the blue-ringed octopus. Of those, the octopus is probably the more deadly. I mean, in the wilds, you actually have to eat a puffer fish to get poisoned. But the octopus actively attacks and stings—that is, injects the poison to kill."

"And the effects?"

"Nausea to begin with."

"And after that?"

"Um... blindness, difficulty breathing leading to heart failure and finally a suffocating death as a result of the paralysis of the diaphragm. And it can happen in just minutes; that is, if you can't get any help."

"Sounds wonderful. Where can you pick up this stuff?"

Wyndham-Smythe shook his head slowly. "Difficult to say, old chap. I'd imagine you could obtain it from some den of iniquity in the more vulgar parts of many a European city."

"Swell," groused Taylor. "But I wonder why they didn't choose something simpler and faster, like cyanide."

The doctor smiled. "Well, you see, old man, if murdering is all you want to do, you're quite correct: cyanide is just the ticket—fast and deadly. However, if you're one of those johnnies who wants to get away and have people think that the death was caused by a heart attack or something like that, then tetrodotoxin's your poison of choice."

"Umm," grunted Taylor thoughtfully. "Just how toxic is this stuff?"

"Very, I'd say. In fact, mixed in the right dosage, it can probably kill off a couple dozen people. Still, it takes its own sweet time to do it. But cyanide? You only need one grain, that's 65 milligrams of hydrogen cyanide, otherwise known as prussic acid, to kill almost instantly. And think, if you put it in solution and into a syringe, you have to be extra careful not to stick yourself which could happen easily. My guess is that's why tetrodotoxin was chosen instead. As for the syringe itself, the bulb type are used for irrigation—you know, for nasal irrigation or for cleaning ears. But those bulbs are larger. This one was much smaller; probably specially made for this purpose."

Taylor nodded. "Thanks, doc. That helps a lot."

"It does?" Wyndham-Smythe shot back, surprised.

"Of course it does. We know a lot more than we knew a couple of days ago. Now we're looking for a medium height, wiry guy who wears Vans and has a stash of specially-made syringes. He's educated to the art of killing as a professional and has the money to spend on a weapon like that knife that's expensive and difficult to find. He's also nondescript because he doesn't mind mingling with crowds where he looks like a nobody. And... he's still on this boat."

"Ship," the doctor shot back.

"Of course," returned Taylor.

"Well, I say. We're farther ahead than I thought we were. But I have to tell you; Captain Drake is very worried about your welfare."

"Does he still have people on me?"

"Of course."

"Good. We've gone mostly through the lengthier part of the cruise. Tomorrow's a travel day, and I don't plan to steer far from the Wells family or places where I'll be easy to spot. We'll just continue steady state."

"Understood," the doctor returned.

Their conversation at an end, the doctor promised to keep the captain updated on what they talked about. Taylor, of course, made no mention of Martin Millner. He decided to wait on that. Then he downed the rest of his latte and went back to his stateroom where he got ready for bed—this time making sure the patio door was properly locked. Then he left a message for Abby who was well into the middle of her work day back home.

Taylor woke up at six feeling like he hadn't rested at all. Still, he was on duty and expected to be handy for Alan at any time of the day. The fact that he was being pursued by a killer didn't matter; he'd signed on to do a job, and do it he would.

At the back of his mind, however, was the gnawing reason why the killer was after him and what he had to do with Ross and Tabby Young. The connection with the sister in L.A. was the most solid one. And it was strange why she dropped him from her case precisely the same day she was murdered. Now, Mott had assured him that the husband, Anson Cameron, had an alibi—witnesses, Mott said. But those could have been bought and paid for. He easily could have had someone else do the deed. The question was why? WHY? Brooke made it clear that her husband was wildly jealous; she also said that they'd worked things out. Yeah, he could have knocked her off himself. Like he said when he saw her, it looked like a rage killing, like someone wanted to get close and personal in eliminating her. He was surprised that Mott let Cameron off so easy because their playbook is so transparent to anyone who knows how the police operate. For them, if the wife is eighty-sixed, the cops always go for the husband as the perp. If it's the girlfriend, the cops always go for the boyfriend as the perp. There had to be a connection he was missing.

Taylor picked up his phone and punched in a number.

"Pierce Investigations," came the voice of Marge who always answered sweetly for customers.

"It's Taylor," he said and could feel the change in disposition without her saying a word.

"Okay," she said wearily, "what is it now?"

"Just a little job that..."

"Jesus Christ!" she spat at him. "You'd think you're the only one I'm supposed to be working for in this goddam..."

"I picked something up for you in Naples," he said to soothe her ire.

"You what?" she replied.

"I said I picked something up for you in Naples. What? You think I don't remember you and all the stuff you do for me?"

"Well..."

"Well, I most certainly do. But if you're gonna treat me like..."

"Wait a minute. Wait a minute," she said. "Okay, I didn't mean it. It's just been a long, hard day, and I didn't find anything new that you asked for."

"That's all right. I have something new that..."

"Something new?" she exclaimed. "Ugh!"

"Marge, this is important. It's the murder of two sisters and an almost husband. That's a whole family. And one of the murders was really ugly; so much so that I can't even tell you about it."

"Okay, okay already. So tell me what you need," she responded with a big sigh.

"All right. The guy's name is Anson Cameron. He's a CPA/high-class accountant type. Is loaded to the gills. His office is in Beverly Hills, but I don't know where. His wife was named Brooke. She was murdered."

"Wait. Wait. Wait. Do you mean the Brooke Cameron I was talkin' about that we had the job with? *She's* the one that was murdered? That Brooke? I talked to her myself when we set up the job. She was really sweet."

"Yeah. That's her."

"Ahh," she gasped. "Why that little sonofabitch!" she exclaimed involuntarily.

"Now, come on. We don't know that he did it; at least not yet. But I've got to know what's up with this guy and if there's any connection to the death of Brooke's sister Tabitha here. So, can you help me with that?" he asked.

"You're damn right I can help you with that," Marge replied as she seemed to come alive with renewed spirit and direction. "I talked to Brooke myself on three or four occasions. She was a really nice person; a sweet girl. And to think that that guy..."

"Hey, we don't know yet."

"Well I do. She told me all about how he used to abuse her, beat her up. This is one case I'll be happy to find everything I can about," she stated demonstratively.

"Good girl!" he replied. "We'll be stopping next in Athens. I'll be thinking of you there too."

"Got it," she replied. "I'll contact you when I get anything at all on that bastard."

"Right!" seconded Taylor and hung up before the earpiece of his phone began smoking from Marge's fit of righteous ire.

But now his mind was abuzz with possibilities, and the single one that rang in his skull was Harry's old adage and solution for ninety percent of the jobs they got: follow the money. Just how that fit into this frame was anyone's guess. Still, if the information he got from Marge was correct, there was some high-stakes dough that passed among this group. He tapped his finger impatiently on the arm of the chair. It was clear he couldn't solve the puzzle now. It was time to get the day rolling.

Taylor snagged his usual breakfast and made some notes on his phone before he went back to pick up and accompany the fam to the breakfast buffet as he always did. He was surprised to hear the excitement of the children and their interest in the museum artifacts that they'd seen the previous day. Alan was somewhat subdued for no reason he could pinpoint. Mandy was her usual talkative self, and Cassandra sat queenlike and nibbled at her breakfast of yoghurt with sprinkles on it as she sipped green tea. She'd probably live forever.

"And how did you like Malta, Taylor?" she asked finally in between nibbles?"

The question was so unexpected that he was caught flatfooted.

"Uh... the shopping part or the museum and cave exploration part?" he responded.

"All of it."

"Well, I'm just an old fashioned math teacher, but my history friend Bud back at school would have gone crazy just seeing those caves. Like the docent said and the brochure described, the caves have been there for untold thousands of years. Imagine; thousands of years."

Alan perked up. "Yeah, I liked that too. Can you imagine what the world will be like in the next forty-thousand years?"

"I doubt that they'll need accountants, dear," put in Cassandra.

The adults chuckled. "And I doubt that they'll be shopping in the stores in Malta," he shot back, to which Cassandra did not laugh.

Since the ship wouldn't reach port for another day, it was like a day of rest when all you had to do was maybe lay around and enjoy the Mediterranean scenery. The whole atmosphere was like something out of a novel or an adventure story.

The sky was cerulean blue, the air temperature was just right, there was the good, clean smell of fresh salt-sea air, and the water was so crystalline clear that in shallower parts you could actually see the sea floor. One could well imagine those seafaring heroes of the Iliad in full armor plying the waves in crafts where the seafoam buffeted the bow as they sailed their way to Troy.

Alan, who wasn't about to fall asleep in the sun again, decided to camp next to the pool while Mandy watched over Curtis. He wanted to play with the new friends he'd made in the last few days. Cassandra took little Amy off to the princess fair and wouldn't rejoin the others for hours. And Taylor? He hung around Alan at a table and played gin while he had a nice latte. All in all, it was a relaxing change from rushing here and there in the ports. It had the makings of a terrific day.

"So, how do you think things are going so far?" asked Alan.

"For you? So far so good. I haven't noticed anyone shoot a hairy eyeball your way. Not even once."

"That's a relief. Then maybe all this protection was for nothing," Alan considered.

Taylor chuckled. "You're right. It's all for nothing—until the second you need it."

Alan nodded. "Okay, I'll be safe rather than sorry. Promise."

"By the way, can I ask what you did that got you into this pickle?"

For a second, Alan considered how he should handle the question. Then he nodded to himself. "See, it's one of those 'I could tell you, but then I'd have to kill you' deals."

Taylor raised his hands defensively. "O-kay, o-kay. I got it."

Alan reconsidered what he'd just said and then blurted out "Aaw, I can tell you without giving away any details."

"Whatever you say," Taylor agreed.

Alan nodded. "Okay, okay, but don't ever tell anyone I told you."

Taylor made a Boy Scout pledge sign.

"So here goes. So you do work for a company for umpteen years, and you just happily do their books, y'know?"

"Got it."

"I mean, they're just numbers; yeah, sometimes big numbers, but they're still just numbers that you add, subtract, etcetera, etcetera, and you see to it that they balance out and everybody gets paid, especially the government."

Taylor nodded agreement.

"Yeah, so everything's hunky dory until one day when you accidentally find that lots of money—and I mean lots—is moving from multiple accounts and banks all over the world to a strange single source you've never heard of before."

Taylor sipped his latte then rubbed his chin meditatively as he listened.

"And when you get around to checking out who is doing the business, you find that it's banks associated with these big-deal entities that are connected to shady mobs, international secret societies, and worldwide religions that all seem to be working in concert for some purpose that little you, sitting in your office in a building in Century City, can't even imagine."

"Really," Taylor put it.

"Yeah, really. But, I mean, you're just an honest broker. You haven't the slightest idea what's going on—and that's okay as long as you just go with the flow."

"And you didn't?"

Alan grunted to himself, unscrewed the cap on his water bottle, and took a big swig. "Stupid, stupid, stupid," he said. "I shoulda let well enough alone, but then I stupidly show the president of one company the accounts and ask him what's up."

"And?"

"Big mistake. First he says shut up and do the work. Then I'm called on the carpet and interrogated in detail like a spy by his board as to what I found."

"And then they didn't need your services anymore and gave you your walking papers."

"Well, it amounted to the same thing. I was scared, I tell ya. But before they could do anything else, a car stops behind mine in the parking garage as I'm leaving work, and these guys—Feds they were—put me in their SUV, drive off, and start telling me horror stories about me and my family if I don't agree to help them. Turns out, they'd been watching that one firm for a long time."

"And then a bunch of clients start dropping you, and you're told that your life won't be worth warm spit if you say anything about the accounts you saw."

"Yeah. That's exactly what I heard."

"But then you leave a message telling everyone that you're loyal to their firm and won't say a word..."

"Yeah, that's right. How'd you know?"

"I'm psychic. And then you decide to get out of Dodge. You contact us for protection, and here we are playing a nice game of gin rummy on deck 11 of the *Flying Cloud.*"

"Yeah that's the story," said Alan as he took another tug off his water bottle. "The Feds said they wouldn't protect me if I didn't play ball. The companies said I'd be toast if I did. There was just no winning."

Taylor looked out across the sea. "Well, there have been no attempts on your life as far as we've gotten, so it looks like your friends are giving you a little leeway because they think you're on their side. They probably have a mole in the Fed's office who substantiates what you said. Meanwhile, the Feds can't do anything. You didn't break any laws... did you?"

"No. None. Ever."

"In that case, unless the Feds want to go to all the trouble of setting up a frame—which is not above those bastards' tricks—then you're probably all right. It's like this: on the one hand, the companies think you know too much to off you while you're in the public eye, while on the other hand the Feds think you're too public to try to bring down. They'd get caught red handed. The result: stalemate."

"You really think so?"

"It's difficult to say. But instead of wringing your hands over it, I'd suggest you just enjoy the present as the family vacation you planned. Let me worry about the no-goodnicks."

Alan chuckled a little. "Thanks, Taylor. That helps. You don't know how I've been worrying. It's not easy thinking you're on someone's hit list."

"Actually, I know exactly how you feel," he said with an understanding Alan couldn't even guess at.

Suddenly Taylor had a thought.

"Uh... the accounting game is a sort of closed club, even in a big town like L.A., isn't it? I mean, everyone knows almost everyone else in the biz. Right?"

"Well... yeah, I guess you could say that. Why do you ask?"

"Have you ever heard of a guy in your business in town named Anson Cameron?"

"What a prick!" Alan replied without hesitation.

"Whoa! Why do you say that?" asked Taylor.

"I'm not going to try to tell you that all CPAs and accountants are angels," he said, "but with Cameron you're talking a real bottom feeder. This is the kind of guy who'd bankrupt his own grandmother if it meant a dime more for himself."

"So he's crooked. Think he's capable of murder?"

Alan thought for a second. "I wouldn't go that far. He's more of a cheap grifter. He'll prey on anyone for a buck. But get personal? I don't know. Why do you ask?"

"Just some stuff that came up with a case. We have to check out everybody."

With that, Taylor changed the subject and suggested another hand of rummy, but Alan was tired and declined.

"Y'know. I don't think anyone can really get me here behind this bulkhead and surrounded by these other parents," he said. "Why don't you and Mandy take a break and get something to eat or something? I'll watch out for Curtis."

"You're sure?" asked Taylor in a serious tone.

"Yeah, I'm sure. Look around. I think I'm safe. Here I am. There's the kid. Come back in a few hours."

"Okay. If you say so. But I'm keeping my phone on. Call if there's anything—and I mean anything you think's suspicious."

Alan nodded, and Taylor walked out from the shade of the big umbrella that covered Alan's table. He stopped by the side of the pool where Mandy was sitting and watching Curtis.

"Hey, Amanda, Alan says we should take a break. He'll keep his eye on Curtis," called out Taylor as he stood at the edge of the pool."

Mandy looked up and shaded her eyes. "You're sure?" she said.

"Hi, Taylor!" interrupted Casey who sat next to another young woman.

Taylor turned to acknowledge Casey. "And this is Anna," she added as she pointed to the other woman.

"Hi, Taylor," said Anna.

"Uh, right," he returned as Anna whispered into Casey's ear: "He's cute," she said, and the two giggled like schoolgirls.

Taylor turned back to Mandy. "Wave to Alan," suggested Taylor. "He'll tell you."

Mandy looked over to Alan who cupped his hands around his mouth and shouted: "Take a break." She nodded back, put an open shirt over her bathing suit, and joined Taylor.

"Where you wanna go? It's a big boat," he said.

"Ship," she corrected.

They chuckled at the little joke.

"Just let me change into my shorts," she said.

"Deal."

"Yeah," seconded Casey. "He can talk to us until you get back," she added as the two girls giggled.

Taylor waited as she changed and talked with the girls about the weather, the pool, and the kids. It only lasted a few minutes until Mandy returned. Then they waved good-bye to the girls and headed for the promenade.

Amanda Bannon was easy to talk to; there was no getting away from that. Like Abby, she was sweet, engaging, and full of life. Taylor felt like a rat for finding her so nice and approachable, but that would be as far as it would go. There was no one else like Abby. They shared an unspoken bond.

Mandy was working on a doctorate in early childhood development at UCLA. Taylor smirked to himself. She could probably watch over Bernstein and his child girlfriend, Kaitlin the mortuary girl, as Marge referred to her. She was planning to teach in a college or university someplace. She didn't owe any debts, owned a steady, reasonable car, and wasn't involved with anyone.

"Relationships take up a lot of time, and lots of times it's time wasted on bickering or what my mother always called flutter."

"Flutter? What's that," he asked.

"Flutter? It's frivolous, wasted talk about inconsequential things—clothes, other people's arguments, political crises you can't do a thing about."

Taylor nodded. Flutter. Precisely what he thought of the world but never articulated it so succinctly.

"I agree completely," he said. "Hey, you're pretty smart," he added.

She smiled with just the slightest look of superiority on her face. "I work at it," she said and then broke out into an infectious laugh as the two happy people continued their walk.

They walked and talked and talked about nothing, just fun stuff Taylor never really had the opportunity to say in his usual role as a licensed private eye who maintained an icy, serious mien because in his world of theft, fraud, and murder, there wasn't much of a chance of it.

They walked the ship's entertainment decks. The one thing you could say about the *Flying Cloud*, like its sister ships *The Shooting Star, The Northern Light, The Golden Fleece,* and *The Windjammer,* was that they really had the details down. People were constantly sweeping any debris off the decks so they were always clean. The venues were invariably spotless and inviting, the food was delicious, the service top notch, and the entertainment excellent. Alan had told Taylor that one of the things that other lines lacked was good entertainment. On those ships often what was offered as a promising event was strictly amateur hour where towards the end of the evening drunken passengers ended up in a conga line that snaked around the pool until people fell in.

Not so the *Flying Cloud's* line of ships. Here everything—especially the live entertainment—was done to the professional level of a Broadway show or the expertise of Six Flags or anything Disney. And that included fireworks.

For the first time in a long time, Taylor felt like he was on holiday. Even with an assassin on his trail, he threw caution to the wind and relaxed like he hadn't in years. He and Mandy went to the kids' arcade where she beat him at pinball three times and he beat her at air hockey. They grabbed burgers for lunch and he even had a strawberry shake—something he couldn't remember doing in years and years. Finally, when the heat became too oppressive, the two of them slipped into one of the ship's movie theaters that played films for adults. It was a rom-com that Taylor was willing to tolerate as long as they could sit in air-conditioned comfort. At length, Mandy fell asleep on Taylor's shoulder. He didn't move, and she stayed until the movie ended, the lights came up, and the people started exiting the theater.

She awoke out of her stupor and felt a bit awkward although Taylor took it in stride. The pair joined the rest of the audience and left the venue to return to Alan and the family.

When they got back to the pool, Alan had been joined by Cassandra, and both kids were splashing in the water. Anna and Casey were nowhere to be seen.

Cassandra smiled cannily with an elongated "We—ell, from the smile on your faces, it looks as though you've had a really good day," she said.

"We did," stated Mandy demonstratively. "I beat him at pinball."

"Did you?" asked Cassandra as a question that was not really a question at all.

"Yeah, she did," seconded Taylor. "I'm not very good at those kinds of games."

"Now, I don't believe that for a second," Cassandra put in.

"I think it's time to get back to our staterooms so we can rest a little before dinner," Alan suddenly interjected. "Mandy..."

"Yes?"

"Please gather the kids and take them upstairs. It's getting late. C'mon Cass."

With that, Alan and Cassandra gathered up their stuff and headed for the elevator. Taylor waved to Mandy who was already gathering up the kids."

"See you at dinner," he said and followed Alan.

When he got back to his cabin, he plunked himself down in the lounge chair and checked his phone. There were messages from Marge, Mott, and Palfrey.

Marge had done a thoroughgoing rundown on the life and doings of Anson Cameron. Her rendition of his biography was filled with snide and snarky asides that revealed her dislike of the man in every sentence. Unfortunately, there was nothing there that even hinted at him as the murderer of his own wife. He'd have to ask her to dig deeper.

Mott didn't have any more information on the murder of Bob Ross, but instead he was interested in what was happening to Taylor and if he had any idea who was after him.

Finally, Palfrey confirmed what the doctor had said, but beyond that, he couldn't add anything new to illuminate the situation.

Taylor sat staring at a wall considering all the stuff he'd put out of his mind during the afternoon. Then he punched in a number on his phone.

Immediately the voice of Theo Mott came on, but it was the outgoing address, not the actual man himself.

"Theo," began Taylor, "you told me last time that Bob Ross died from poisoning, but you didn't tell me how or what kind of poison was used. Could you forward me that information in a message or e-mail?" he requested. Then he hung up. Time to rest up a little before going to dinner.

Alan buzzed him at the usual appointed time for pick up, and he joined the fam as they made their way to their reserved table. Once seated, Taylor looked furtively about the room and noticed that Mr. Kaiser across the way was waving hello at him. Taylor waved back.

"Who's that?" inquired Cassandra.

Taylor chuckled. "An old seaman I ran into at the coffee bar. He's a nice old fellow who can really spin some fantastic yarns."

"I guess you never know who you'll run into on this tub," said Alan. "Anyway, the point is to have fun. Just look at Amy, our little princess."

Indeed, little Amy was dressed in a pretty—and pretty expensive—princess dress. She was also wearing makeup and had had her hair done professionally. Taylor could only think of the sad case of JonBenet Ramsey—one of those little kids who was unlucky enough to be introduce into the adult world all too early.

"Doesn't Amy look beautiful?" crowed the mother as she smiled at each person around the table.

"Yes, beautiful," replied Taylor as he sat there thinking more's the pity, let the kid have a childhood fer chrissakes.

The rest of the dinner went off without a hitch. Afterward, Mandy would take the children to one of their cartoon movies while the adults went to one of the nightclubs.

This evening the nightclub had a magician act. The fellow could do all sorts of tricks with cards and other props in addition to psychic tricks and clairvoyant readings of people's lives. The "fun" part of the performance is when he hypnotized audience members and had them do silly things that weren't too embarrassing but gave everyone a good-natured laugh.

The evening was capped off at around 9 p.m. The nightclub act was over, and the kids were returned to their parents.

Everyone gathered on the upper decks at the rails as the ship's crew set off an amazing quarter-hour's worth of fireworks to the melodic strains of popular themes played by a grand orchestra piped throughout the ship that musically punctuated each explosion in the sky. Everyone looked to the heavens and at the amazing pyrotechnic display that only fun parks usually exhibited. Nonetheless, the whole thing made the evening all that more magical.

At the end, Alan and Cassandra started to pull their kids in the direction of the elevator.

"C'mon kids. Time for bed."

"All right, daddy," said Amy and Curtis together as they took their hands and began walking.

Taylor was still at the rail and just turned Alan's way when Mandy swooped in and planted a sustained kiss full on his lips. It stunned him, but he didn't push her away. Instead, she released silently and followed after the family while Taylor caught his bearings standing there.

What the hell was that, he thought to himself as he felt his lips with his fingers. He could still taste her lipstick and the fragrance of her skin lingered with him for a second.

Then he remembered where he was and what he was about, shook it off, and walked quickly to catch up to Alan.

Six a.m. came way too early the next day. Taylor had had a restless night, and his sleep was only half a sleep. It seemed that he was half awake through the night. Whatever it was, he didn't feel like a happy camper this particular morning.

Actually, that wasn't what raised his ire; it was the fact that his phone had gone off even before his alarm went off. It was Mott.

"Morning, bright eyes," the man said as a greeting.

"Do you know what time it is?" groused Taylor.

"Of course. I looked it up. You're about nine hours ahead of us."

"You coulda waited."

"Naw, I was just headin' out of the office, and I saw your message," declared Mott. "It sounded like you wanted the info right away."

"Well, not right away but..."

"S'okay. I got it covered, so lemme tell you what I know. It seems that Mr. Ross was injected with poison while he was in his seat in the airplane. Think about it: he had an aisle seat, he fell asleep. It would have been easy to give him a quick injection. He never would have awakened."

"Um," grunted Taylor. "So what was the poison?" he asked.

"Uhh... It was... it was... I got it right over here. Wait a second while I find the folder."

"Was it tetrodotoxin by any chance?" he asked.

"Yeah, it was. Tetrodotoxin. How the hell did you know that?" Mott asked, surprised.

"Because I'm assuming the same guy tried the same thing on me. Fortunately, he missed and left the evidence."

"Well, I'll be damned!" exclaimed Mott.

"Better than me being dead. By the way, just an FYI. The perp uses little bulb syringes that hold just enough liquid to do the job. They look specially made. You might see if the Barcelona police found one of these—maybe on the plane. Anyway, it's gotta be the same guy who attacked me, and he's gotta be on this boat. So, if I were you, I'd have the authorities go over the airplane's manifest and this ship's manifest with a fine-tooth comb to see if you can turn him up."

"We already have. So far the only suspicious character we've found is..."

"Yes?"

"You!"

"Funny," Taylor replied. "You'll have to do better than that."

"From here?" whined Mott. "Like I told you; if you could just get me a ticket to join you, this would all be so much simpler, and we could wrap it up together."

"Thanks, but I think you'd do better to see the chaplain and get your TS card punched."

Mott laughed like hell. "Okay, okay, smart guy. Just don't forget to inform me after the guy's offed you."

"You can count on it," he replied and rang off.

Taylor ran his hand through his hair. The guy had missed killing him with the knife. It was just a fluke that he missed with the poison. Hopefully, a third attempt wouldn't be the charm. And today there'd be big crowds where they were going. He'd have to be extra careful for Alan, of course, but also for himself.

Taylor made it down to the buffet at his usual time and loaded his plate with its usual fare. He fleetingly thought that he was getting used to these scrumptious breakfasts and that he'd probably miss them a lot once he returned home.

He sat at his usual spot and went through the itinerary for the day as he ate. This would be a difficult day, he reckoned, since they'd be going places packed with people—precisely the kind of place where the assassin could get up close and personal and stick you with one of those poison syringes almost without being noticed. The only way around that was to make sure that Alan and the fam stuck together and avoided getting too close to anyone who was not part of the family.

Breakfast complete, he headed back to his stateroom and noticed on the way that the ship was just pulling into the port at Pireaus. He could see the line of busses that were poised to take the tourists to their destinations in Athens and environs.

Once in his cabin he phoned Palfrey to see if any progress had been made on identifying the killer. Palfrey acknowledged that they had been in contact with the authorities at Barcelona a couple days after they were informed about Bob Ross' death. Tabby Young's death, of course, increased their awareness tenfold. But there was no real way they could pinpoint the suspect. They weren't the police, and they didn't have the wherewithal to investigate the background of every passenger on board. The police were the ones to do that, or maybe INTEPOL that had records on people worldwide covering everything from sex abuse to murder, and they too were on the case.

Taylor walked out to his balcony and sat down. It only now crossed his mind that the sisters were murdered rather savagely while Ross was killed in a different way as he almost was too. Interesting. But why? Just then the ship's horn blew. It was time to get ready to see the sights.

The family could take its time with breakfast since Alan had, as always, taken care to have a private limo on hand to whisk the fam to all of the favored tourist locations well ahead of the other folks on board. They had to settle for the ship tours of Athens which took a long time to arrange and then participate in. With a bit more time on their side, the fam could return to their cabins at a more leisurely pace to pick up backpacks, hats, sunscreen, and anything else needed for their next adventure and still beat the other tourists to the venues.

Taylor suggested that they head first thing directly for the Acropolis not only to beat the crowds but to see the Parthenon while it was still the cooler part of the day. Cassandra thought that was a wonderful idea. She, of course, had a list of shops that sold yet more tchotchkes that she wanted to visit, but that could wait. Of the big-ticket items on the tourist list was not just the Parthenon, but also the Agoura with Hephaistos' temple and the Archeological Museum. Taylor suggested they see those first.

Taylor's assumption concerning the tourists had been correct. Led by their chauffeur and tour guide, Dimitrios, the family climbed the hill to the top of the Acropolis. There stood the famous Parthenon with its columns reaching into the sky but looking a bit worse for wear after the couple thousand years since they were first erected. The kids ran around the thing while the adults listened to Dimitrios' patter about its construction and history among other asides. For example, he pointed to a spot on one of the columns in front where Lord Byron had carved his name although it was difficult to make out since others had done the same thing. Tourists from another group strained their necks to see what Dimitrios was pointing at which aggravated the tour docent. He also made a point of explaining that the famous Elgin marbles that had been taken by the English and were now in the British Museum might be repatriated since talks were being held between the nations concerning these important artifacts. Again, the other tourists listened to him to the chagrin of the docent who then hurried the group off to another part of the monument.

At this hour of the day, the air was still cool and fresh. And you only needed to turn to see the amazing, vast vista of the city that lay at the feet of the monument in every direction like a fantastic carpet made up of a jumble of rooftops.

The foot-traffic in the Agoura was picking up when the family finally arrived to see the actual spot where Socrates used to spar with the sophists, influenced—and some said corrupted—the youth of Athens, and where he sealed his own doom and was essentially forced to swallow hemlock.

Hephaistos' temple was really something to see, since it was still in excellent shape and gave the viewer a better impression of what a Greek temple looked like in a less ravaged condition.

Amazing too was the National Museum that housed the art of Athenian antiquity including its wonderful statuary and particularly the bronze statue of Poseidon poised with a missing trident he was about to hurl. For Cassandra, that together with the famous Antikythera mechanism were the highlights of the visit. She had wanted to go to the temple site of Delphi, the site of the oracle where they could explore the hilltop ruins, the amphitheater, and Temple of Apollo, but that was a full-day tour, and they didn't have the time.

Consequently, Cassandra announced that she now wanted to go shopping with her list. Alan, knowing what drudgery this was likely to entail after their last trip to the shops in Malta, suggested that Dimitrios take Cass wherever she wished to go and help her with her shopping while he and the others would take one of the red Hop-On-Hop-Off Bus Tours that ran all day. The busses went all over the city and even down to the Beach Riviera where the kids could run around and expend some of their pent up energy. That being agreed upon as well as the time and location where they would reconnect, the fam split up and went their separate ways.

The red tour busses were double-decker, open air affairs which were a lot of fun, especially for the kids who ran up and down the aisle while Alan, Mandy, and Taylor took in the sights. Neither of them mentioned the kiss, and it was as though it had never happened which was all to the good as far as Taylor was concerned. Just more flutter not worth mentioning, he mused to himself.

As relaxing as the day had been thus far, Taylor was on the alert every second which caused a lot of inner stress since he had to constantly check out the environment from every side every second. Nonetheless, he felt comfortable about what they were doing since it would be difficult for an assassin to follow their un-planned moves. That would work at least until they got back to the ship where their activities followed a more or less prescribed routine.

They returned to the Agoura where they were set to meet at around 4 o'clock when Cassandra should have completed her shopping spree. But she was late. While they waited, Alan watched the kids run around on the grass. About twenty minutes later the limo drove up, and Dimitrios jumped out to open the doors for the new passengers that were looking the worse for wear as did Dimitrios. Cassandra must have run him ragged.

Meanwhile, she couldn't stop talking about her shopping trip through the Plaka District and the many buys she made. The best of these was at the shop of Nikos Nicolaides who dealt in flokatis—beautiful white rugs made from sheep skins. Of course, Dimitrios had his hands full taking all of Cassandra's purchases from the shops to the car, but he managed. As with the other drivers that Alan had hired, Dimitrios would see to it that all of her goods would be carefully wrapped, packaged, and sent to their home address in Brentwood. Cassandra let out a big sigh but was nonetheless elated as though she'd just put in a full day working at a steel mill.

The limo made its way back to the dock. The family debarked and then got on board again, swiping their ID cards and dragging themselves to their quarters.

And once again, they were at the most dangerous part of the trip—when an attacker could get to them; them being Alan and Taylor.

Everyone was taking their usual rest before dinner. Taylor dropped himself into the lounge chair in his suite and pulled out his phone. He punched in a number.

"Hello," came the familiar reply.

"Hi, it's me," said he.

"Oh, it is, is it! You've taken your old sweet time getting back to me."

"You know that's not true. You were working. I left you messages."

"Not the same as speaking with you. It upsets my day if we don't talk."

"Does it? Does it really?"

"Well, I do get a little perturbed."

"S'okay. Take it out on the people at work."

"Ha. Ha. They're a lot nicer than you."

"Everyone's a lot nicer than I am. You know what a miserable individual I can be. Just ask Marge at work. She'll tell you."

"And are you Mr. Grumpy on your job on the ship?"

"Oh, here? Naw, can't do it. Here I have to be mister nice guy personified. It's part of my act. The result is everyone loves me. Especially the women."

"Oh, really? Any make a pass at you?"

"Only one so far."

"What? She didn't kiss you, did she?"

"As a matter of fact she did. And it's funny, she is my type of girl, but you know what the trouble is?"

"No, I don't, and I don't think I want to," she returned, obviously miffed.

"Well, the thing is, I've already got a girl. The best one around. The only one-of-a-kind original Abby there is."

Abby was silent for a second. "You're not just kidding me, are you?"

"Oh, I expect you know I'm not."

"You're always so sure of yourself and arrogant."

"Yep. Can't help it. That's who I am, and that's also why you like me so much."

"Hm," she grunted. "I'm going to have to think that over."

"You do that, sweets. Meanwhile I've got to get a little rest. I'm on the duty roster for the dinner and night entertainment detail."

"It sounds like you're having way too much fun."

"Well, the food's certainly good. But naw, too much fun for me probably would be getting nineteen repealed."

"You're impossible."

"My greatest asset. Except for the fact that you don't mind being connected with me."

"Maybe I do."

"I'll guess I'll have to ask you again after I get back home and lay one on you when you open the door."

"You're impossible."

"And you're repeating yourself. I'll call tomorrow. I don't want you to be perturbed. I prefer you healthy, hearty and scrappy—and, don't forget, I never stop thinking about you."

"Oh, Taylor. Come home soon."

"Just a few more days. Keep busy, and I'll be there before you know it."

"Call tomorrow?"

"You know I will."

Taylor rang off and sat contemplating just precisely what he *was* doing. He couldn't wait for this job to be over.

CHAPTER 8

Dinner was its usual scrumptious occasion. The family was still wiped out from the day's touring, so no one spoke a lot. Cassandra asked what Alan and the kids had seen and done. No one asked what she had seen or done—but she kept talking about it anyway.

The meal over, the parents decided to see the live play at the ship's Grand Theater. On tonight's calendar was their rendition of *West Side Story* with a full orchestra backup and a good cast that didn't include a predominance of Latins because it was just a musical.

Harry once got on his high horse when Marge started defending the idea of cultural and ethnic appropriation. He explained that people in places like Japan, Russia, France, and Germany had regularly put on productions of *West*

Side Story, Julius Caesar, Madame Butterfly, Waiting for Godot, and any number of plays and musicals in their own languages since like forever. And guess what? Nobody ever complained that those foreign actors using their foreign tongue were pretending that they were somebody else from a different culture. So much for those freakin' woke idiots whining about ethnic appropriation! That seemed to shut Marge up—which was something of a rarity in the office.

Fortunately, none of that came up during the performance of the musical as Alan, Cassandra, and Taylor sat and enjoyed it while the kids were enjoying yet another cartoon adventure with Mandy who probably wasn't.

After the play ended, Taylor waited for the crowd to disperse, and then he accompanied Alan and Cassandra out of the theater. Mandy was waiting for them outside with the kids, both of whom were out on their heels. Alan picked up the sleeping Amy, and Taylor picked up Curtis. The whole family went as one to the elevator and to their digs on their deck.

"Want to get something to drink?" Mandy asked after Taylor had deposited Curtis on his bed. "It'll just take me a minute to get them in their jammies and tuck them in."

"Uh, okay. I can use a latte," he said. "You aren't bringing your friends Anna or Casey with you, are you?" he asked.

She laughed curtly. "Of course not," she replied.

"Then fine," he agreed. "I'll be waiting outside."

Taylor waited at the far end of the corridor near the elevator. It didn't take but a few minutes for Mandy to finally appear. The pair got on the elevator and took it to deck 12.

They took their seats at the coffee bar. An unfamiliar barista, smiled at Taylor.

"Can I help you sir?" he asked with a Midland's accent.

"Where's Mike?" he asked.

"Oh, he's probably on deck eleven at the ice cream concession. They move us around quite a bit. I'm Tommy."

"Huh. Alright, Tommy, in that case I'll have a latte, and the lady will have..."

"English breakfast tea with cream and sugar," she said.

Tommy put a creamer and a little bowl of sugar cubes before her. She prepared her tea and sipped at it delicately.

"Good?" asked Taylor.

"Um. Delicious."

"Yes, it's good to sit back and review the day with a nice warm beverage, don't you think?"

"Actually, I was wondering why you didn't mention that kiss all day?" she said as she looked over the edge of her cup at him mid-sip.

Taylor chuckled. "Because I didn't reckon it to be anything important. I thought that you just got caught up in the atmosphere of the evening. It happens."

"Not to me. Does this kind of thing happen to you all the time? Maybe from your Margaret Pepper?"

Taylor laughed out loud. "Margaret Pepper. That's rich," he said. "Never even thought of kissing her. You know..." he began but was cut off.

"Taylor. Good evening," a man said as he took a seat at the bar.

"Mr. Kaiser," he returned as the old man settled in.

"I'll have an espresso," said Kaiser to the barista.

"Yes sir, replied Tommy as he made up the brew and set it before the old man who started spooning in sugar.

"Mr. Kaiser," said Taylor, "I'd like you to meet Amanda. She's the nanny to my cousin's kids."

Kaiser coughed a little and nodded congenially. "Nice meeting you. It's good to know that other denizens of the night have to decompress after a day of playing tourist in the company of a couple thousand people. It's murderous. Especially for someone my age."

"I can imagine," she said and then turned to Taylor. "I have to be up early, so I'll leave you two to discuss the cares of the day," she put in.

"Please don't go on my account," urged Kaiser.

"I'm not," she replied casually. "I'm just very tired and have no time for flutter. Nice meeting you, Mr. Kaiser. Good night," she said as she got off her stool and headed for the elevator.

"Flutter? What is flutter?" asked Kaiser after she was out of sight.

"Inconsequential talk."

"Ah, yes. I agree."

"That was some wild story you told me, you know," said Taylor.

"I was all true nonetheless."

"And you know Beatrice Jolly?"

"Let's save that discussion for another time," said the old man.

"Sure," replied Taylor and then tried to think of something else to say to buoy the conversation, such as it was. "Uh... well, just a couple more islands to go."

"Yes," returned Kaiser.

"Then it's back to the workaday world."

"Well, I'm retired and have been for many years. But after having dealt with the crowds and the compressed time frame for visiting each city on this cruise, I can tell you that I might be very happy to be back home," concluded Kaiser as he finished his espresso and awkwardly slipped off his stool. "Perhaps we can meet up again in a couple of days," he said.

"My pleasure," returned Taylor, and the old man smiled and walked off.

After getting ready for bed, Taylor flopped on top of his covers and checked his phone for messages and e-mails. There was still nothing from Marge or Mott. Palfrey also hadn't contacted him yet either. Jesus! How long could it take him to run a computer check on the ship's manifest? The guy had to be there, and they had to have some kind of background information on him that he could get Mott to drill down on.

He switched off his phone.

This case was making him crazy. If the killer was just trying to get Alan, that was one thing. But since he was also a target, that was something else. If Brooke Cameron was the connection, why all this? His contact with her had been completely straightforward and all at her instigation. She hired him through the firm. He set her up in the hotel to make sure she was away from her husband. She didn't tell him nothin'; she didn't give him nothin'. There was no hidden money involved. There was no secret information involved. That was it.

His phone buzzed. It was Palfrey.

"Yeah?" Taylor answered.

"We were finally able to check out your man with the Vans."

"And?"

"And he's a British citizen who lives in Delaware and is a stock broker. That's all we have for now."

Taylor tapped his finger impatiently. "He wears Vans," he repeated impatiently.

"We've found a number of people on board who wear Vans. None of them look suspicious."

"But he's the only one who has any connection to me."

Palfrey sighed. "Well, sorry sir, but there's nothing else to add here," he concluded.

Taylor's mouth tightened. "Okay, Palfrey," he said finally. "I'll get back to you."

With that he punched in Mott's e-mail and left a description of Ardie and what he had learned from Palfrey. He wanted all he could get on the guy. Then he dropped his phone on the nightstand and switched on the TV. He found an old black and white episode of Perry Mason and watched the program until he got sleepy and dozed off.

It was six o'clock in the morning before he knew it. He blinked at the ceiling as he opened his eyes and got his bearings. Oh, yeah. another Greek port. Uh, this one was uh... Mykonos. Right. He wondered if it had a lot of shopping opportunities for the missus. Whatever. He hopped out of bed and got the day rolling.

Mandy wasn't at the buffet, not that he expected her, but she seemed a bit frosted when she parted company with him the previous evening. He was just shoveling his eggs onto his plate when he heard someone call his name. It was Mandy's friends Anna and Casey who were all bubbly and energetic.

"Hi, Taylor. Do you always eat here this early?" Casey asked.

"Yeah, it's a little quieter," he responded, "but I haven't seen you folks here before."

"No, we just wanted to try and beat the crowd. Personally, I'm getting tired of fighting for space all day long," she complained.

Taylor chuckled commiseration.

"Are you going into town today?"

"Yeah, the whole family is. Mandy too."

"I think she's a little miffed with you," Anna ventured.

"With me? What did I do?" he asked.

Casey smiled from ear to ear. "That's just it, silly," she said with a big grin. "You didn't do anything. See you around, Taylor," she added and the pair walked off across the room to a table where a clutch of women were eating together.

Taylor parked himself at his usual table and started in on his breakfast. He was in the middle of it when he thought of something else that Marge could look up. He took out his phone and punched in.

"Marge," he said after she picked up, "it's me."

"Oh, my God, Taylor. It's just awful."

"Huh? What are you talking about?"

"Didn't Harry call you? He was supposed to."

"About what?" he asked.

"We were burgled."

"Burgled? For what? Divorce papers?" he returned with a chuckle.

"I don't know. All I know is that when I came in yesterday morning, the place was completely torn apart. Bernstein and I have spent the last whole day putting things back together."

"So, what was stolen?"

"We haven't got a clue. To tell you the truth it doesn't look like they got away with much except maybe for Harry's expensive cameras and a couple of office guns that he had in a little safe in his closet. They took the whole safe."

"You called the cops, of course."

"Of course, but a big lot of help they were. We had to fill out reams of forms on the date, the approximate time of the burglary, what was taken, etcetera, etcetera, etcetera. At least I was able to give them the serial numbers off the guns from my computer files. But like that's gonna help!"

Taylor sighed. "Man, just what we needed!"

"Yeah, sorry I haven't been able to get any farther into your stuff, but I'm up to my ears here."

"No, no. I understand," he said. "Just keep getting the office in shape. That'll be the best for now. Get back to my search when you can."

"I promise. You still going to bring me that stuff from Italy?" she asked a little sheepishly.

"Yeah, of course I am," he replied with a laugh.

"Oh, oh, I almost forgot..." she added.

"What?"

"Your package..."

"My what?"

"Your package. Luckily I gave it to Bernstein to drop off at your friend Abby's before all this happened."

Taylor went stone cold silent.

"Taylor?"

"What was the return address and name?"

"Uh..." said Marge as she searched her memory. "Oh, yeah. It was weird. There wasn't a name; just an address. It was Crescent Drive and Sunset, #5," she said as she enunciated each word. "That help?"

Silence.

"Taylor? You still there?"

"Uh, yeah. Thanks, Marge. Listen, if Bernstein checks in, tell him to call me immediately. I'll try to get in touch with him."

"Uh... sure, will do, bubbie," she replied and was going to say good-bye, but he'd already hung up.

Taylor quickly punched in Bernstein's home number.

"Hi, I'm not in right now, but..." the outgoing message answered.

He hung up and punched in Bernstein's cell number.

"Hello?" Bernstein answered.

"This is Taylor. Marge said..."

"Taylor. Man, you wouldn't believe what happened at the office. When Marge got in yesterday morning..."

"I know. I know all about it. Listen to me..."

"Marge told you?" said Bernstein.

"Yeah, she did," Taylor confirmed. "She also said she gave you a package for me that you were going to give to Abby."

"I'm sorry, Taylor. I just haven't had time yet to deliver..."

"That's okay. That's okay," said Taylor, relieved. "I don't want you to give it to Abby. Instead, I want you to take it to Barney Paisley at his restaurant, and tell him to lock it up in his safe. Got that? Take it to Barney, and tell him lock it up in his safe."

"Uh, okay. Whatever you say."

"That's the ticket, Bernstein. See you when I get back. I owe you a dinner."

"A dinner? Can I bring Kaitlin along as..."

"Not a problem. Now get that package to Barney pronto. Hand it to him personally."

"Will do, Taylor," promised the lad.

With that, Taylor hung up. Then he quickly punched in another number. It rang and rang and rang. Finally, they answered.

"Hello?" came Abby's voice.

Taylor let out an audible sigh. "Man, you almost gave me a heart attack."

"What? Taylor?"

"Yeah, it's me. Are you at work right now?"

"Yes. Why? What's going on?"

"Sweetheart, I don't have the time to explain, but please do as I say as quickly as you can."

"Do what?"

"I want you to get in your car, drive to the airport, park in the monthly parking, and get on a flight to your parents' just as fast as you can. Don't tell anyone where you're going."

Abby chuckled, "Are you crazy? Is this a joke. What are you doing, Taylor?" she laughed a little more.

"If murder were funny, I'd be joking, but I'm not."

"Huh?"

"Look. You need to get out of town just as fast as you can. Make up something at work. Tell them you've come down with the flu or something. But you've got to get away now."

"Taylor. Be serious."

"I am serious, Abby," he pressed. "There are some people out there who won't stop at anything to get at me, and if that means going through you, they'll do it. They've already murdered three people."

Abby was suddenly silent. Taylor waited for a response.

"Abby? Abby, you still there?"

"Yes. All right. I'll do just as you say."

"Good girl. Message me all along the way. I'll get back to you. And whatever you do, do not go back to the apartment. Understand? Don't go back there."

"Okay, okay. I'll leave now."

"I'll get back to you as soon as I can. Stay safe."

"I will. Bye."

Abby hung up, and as soon as she did, Taylor punched in another number. It was Mott's number. He answered right away.

"Theo? This is Taylor. Listen. Don't talk. I've come into some more information. Our Hollywood office was burgled. I have reason to believe that the people who burgled Pierce Investigations' offices are the same people who murdered Brooke Cameron—I'm pretty sure they're going to turn over my apartment and Abby Hart's place if they haven't already done so."

"What?" Mott answered incredulously.

"Could you please check it out?"

"You want us to put Abby in protective custody?"

"No. For now, just check our apartments and get back to me. That's all I need."

"Man, half a world away and..."

"Yeah, I hear you. Thanks for your help, Theo. I hope it's nothing, but I fear that you'll find..."

"Don't worry," Mott assured him. "I'll check it out, and I'll get back at you at this number."

"Thanks, Theo. Thanks a lot," said Taylor and then rang off.

Only one more call to make. He punched in a bunch of numbers on his phone and waited.

"Barney's. Paul speaking," came the answer.

"Paul, This is Taylor. Is Barney there?"

"Yeah, yeah. Hey, where you been? You haven't been by for a steak in about a week. What gives?"

"Work. I'm out of town. Anyway, can I speak with..."

"Hang on. He's eating his lunch. Just a sec."

Paul went off to get Barney. Taylor could hear Miles' "Green Dolphin Street" playing in the background, the muffled conversation of customers, and the jingle of silverware as they ate. Suddenly, somebody came on the line.

"Hey, are you back already? I didn't expect you for maybe a..."

"Barn, listen. I've got a problem."

Barney gave an exasperated sigh. "Why call me whenever you've got trouble? Why don't you call that cop friend of yours and then call me when only good stuff happens?"

"Because you're my best friend?"

That stopped Barney dead in his tracks.

"Okay, what is it this time?"

Taylor told Barney the whole story about the cruise, the murders, the attacks, and especially about the package and the danger that attached to it.

"You don't know what's in it?" Barney asked.

"I don't want you getting mixed up in this thing. I thought you could just lock it in your safe until I got back."

"What makes you think the bad guys won't know I have it? Wouldn't it be better if we knew what this was all about?"

Taylor was torn. He'd rather not have yet another friend become a target because of this case. On the other hand, if they knew what it was all about now, maybe the solution would be more apparent.

"Okay, you're right. You look at it. But can you also scan whatever's in there and send me a PDF? Then we can discuss it together."

"Not a problem."

"Okay. Bernstein is going to bring it to you any time today."

"I'll be here."

"And be careful. That shot in the butt you got a few years back isn't anything next to what these guys are capable of."

Barney laughed darkly. "Don't forget what I used to do in the corps. Because I can still do it."

"Yeah, you can, Sergeant Major," seconded Taylor. "I'll be waitin' to hear from ya."

He hung up the phone, sat back, and tried to contemplate everything that just happened in the last twenty minutes.

Recognizing the address Marge recited, the package had to have come from Brooke Cameron, and she must have sent it from the hotel before she was murdered. That much of the case was now clear. What wasn't clear was how her sister and the others were involved. As for the attacks on himself, the bad guys obviously believed that Taylor already knew what was in the package, and he had to be shut up—like Tabitha and Bob Ross were shut up. So, yeah, it would be better if he at least knew what this whole thing was about, and to find out, Barney had to crack it open.

How long that would take, he didn't know. What he did know was that he still had a job to do. He had to pick up the family for breakfast, and then they'd all see the new location for the day: Mykonos. This excursion couldn't have come at a worse time.

On his way up to gather the family, he could see two other cruise ships already anchored in the harbor and shuttles transporting people to the island.

Cassandra had already been schooled about Mykonos by her friend Joy and had already drawn up her plans for the day. The island was once a reserve of sorts for the elite in the seventies but had gradually lost its charm for the next generation of rich people. Thus, it was chock-full of little allées and lanes where one could walk among shops filled with low end Greek kitsch on the one hand and high end *haut couture* on the other. Cassandra said she wasn't much interested in buying anything—except perhaps for trinkets for her friends. Otherwise, there were a number of beaches and beach resorts where tourists camped out on lounges shaded by big umbrellas while they relaxed and read, sunbathed, or drank the exotic libations that flowed unendingly from the bar. Meanwhile, Mandy, Amy, and Curtis would stay on board and avail themselves of the entertainments that were designed for kids—the water slides, the arcades, fun clubs, dessert diners, and the movies and cartoon shows.

While the rest of the tourists had to take the little shuttles to the island, Alan had already chartered a speed boat and guide to help them through the day.

As usual, they beat the vast majority of tourists to the island while it was still fairly early and cool. The town itself looked to have been there since time immemorial. It was a sea of whitewashed stucco houses with powder-blue trim where colorful and fragrant red, blue, and yellow flowers bloomed everywhere. The inviting little lanes coursed this way and that all over the town with unique little shops around every corner.

Cassandra stopped in a number of these and bought the trinkets that she planned to give to her friends. By early afternoon, the group was tired of walking and headed for the family friendly Pasaji Beach Club. Their guide, Niko, made sure they had comfortable lounge chairs. The waitress was on them before they knew it. Cassandra pulled out a book to read while Alan and Taylor pulled out a deck of cards. The management kept a constant stream of mellow music going to accompany the ever-flowing libations while the guests relaxed.

While it seemed a shame to waste the opportunity to explore the island in more detail, the sad fact was that there actually wasn't much to see on Mykonos that was all that interesting. Sure, there was the town and the old windmills that had been there for countless years but were no longer in use—their bare arms stabbing the sky like bicycle spokes. There were other beaches that were sans entertainment and within driving distance that provided quiet and solitude. But most of the island's landscape was dry, barren, and unappealing unless you were a desert rat.

Across the bay was the island of Delos, that ancient trading center and religious site that was known as the birthplace of Apollo and Artemis. It was where a number of the artifacts now in the Athens Museum had been found. But now the town was mostly a pile of ruins on a dry, brown landscape and mostly interesting only to souls who had a penchant for mythology and archeology.

Meanwhile, Taylor found the environs of the Pasaji Beach Club perfect for his needs. Because the lounges were all set some distance apart from each other, he could easily keep an eye on Alan while they played cards and while Alan took a brief dip in the ocean. More than that, the Wi-Fi was great.

By mid-afternoon both Alan and Cassandra had nodded off. Fortunately, the pair were lying on lounges that were completely covered by large umbrellas so there would be no repeat of the sunburn episode. Taylor stayed awake and checked his phone from time to time, but there was nothing new on it yet. A couple of times he almost nodded off but caught himself and picked up Cassandra's book to read just to stay awake.

About an hour later he got an e-mail from Mott. Yeah, his apartment had been ransacked. If there was something missing, he'd have to wait to see when he came back to town. Abby's place, however, hadn't been touched which gave Taylor hope that they didn't know about her—which was something of a great relief.

The next message came from Barney who also had sent an e-mail with four PDFs attached to it along with a cryptic message to look the stuff over and then to call him back when he could. Taylor hungrily opened up the attachment as fast as he could and then switched from one page to another.

"What the hell is this!" he exclaimed out loud as he flipped back and forth among the pages in befuddlement.

In truth, there was nothing very obvious about what he'd been sent. All the pages were printed in 8 point Ariel sans serif. At the top left was the designation No. DP216/1—whatever the hell that meant. Across the top of the page were large columns designated Part Cat, Number, Tools and Universal Parts. Down the pages were headings in alphabetical order designated Body/Lamp Assembly. Cooling, Electrical, Engine, Fuel and Air, Exhaust, Ignition, Suspension, Transmission, Supplemental.

It was an auto parts list like the ones he'd been handed every time Ricky Villereal repaired one of the cars he managed to destroy. But really! This was it? This was worth the lives of three people? There had to be more to it than that; there just had to be.

Right at that moment, Cassandra woke up from her nap and looked around at the people on the beach.

"I must have fallen asleep," she said.

Taylor shut off his phone. "Well, that's easy to do on these lounges. I dozed off myself."

"What time is it?" she asked.

Taylor checked his watch. "Probably about time we started to get back. Our shipmates have been leaving to catch the shuttle, but we've still got time to catch a snack and a drink before we take the speeder back to the ship. Wanna do that?"

"Sounds like a great idea," said she and nudged Alan. "Hey, sleepy head," she called. "Time to get up."

Alan woke up groggy, yawned like a savannah lion, and looked around. "Boy, was that a good nap," he said.

"For me too, but Taylor says we should start getting back to the boat."

Alan rubbed his stomach. "I'm a little hungry."

"That's okay," Taylor put in. "We can get a snack before we take the speedboat back, and once back on the ship you can hit all of the eating joints you like."

"Deal!" agreed Alan enthusiastically.

They snacked at a little joint on the quay and had chit-chat where they could watch the boats in the harbor. Cassandra repeated what she'd heard about their next stop from her friend Joy and the plans she'd already made. Alan munched some fries, drank his beer, and kept his mouth shut. Taylor strained to make himself look interested in what she was saying.

It was the end of the day, and the sun was low in the sky by the time they got into the speedboat back to the ship. As per usual, they checked in with their ID cards. Taylor escorted them back to their stateroom where Cassandra asked if he'd go check out the kids and bring them back to rest before dinner. Taylor agreed and went on his way even though he couldn't wait to get back and call Barney about the stuff he'd sent.

He phoned Mandy who reported that she and the kids were just getting out of one of their movies at the Magic Theater, and he could meet them there. It only took a couple of minutes to get to the venue where a mob of screaming kids were running out of the place. He spotted Mandy and the kids near the tail end of the mob. They looked energized, she looked ragged.

"Oh, my God," she said when they finally met. "They never stop talking and making noise in the theater. I think my brain is rattling from side to side. My ears are ringing."

Taylor chuckled. "And did I get an earful from Cassandra today. If I have to hear what her friend Joy has said, done, will do, will think, just one more time, I think I'll go batty," he declared.

"Okay, then it's a draw," Mandy supposed.

"Anyway, they sent me down to see what the little rug rats were up to and to corral them back to rest up before dinner."

"I can use that," she agreed.

"Great!" he exclaimed.

But she hesitated. "Uh, Taylor?"

"Yeah?"

"I wanted to apologize for my behavior."

"There's nothing to apologize for."

"For me there is. I never act that way. I don't know what came over..."

He stopped, smiled, and placed his hands on her shoulders. "Amanda, look, you're a really good person. I watch how you take care of the kids and everything else. The main thing is—it's clear that your heart's in the right place. You've got nothing to be sorry for."

It took only a couple of minutes to get Mandy and the kids back to their cabin. Taylor got into his room as soon as he could and punched in a number on his phone.

"Barney, it's me," he said.

"You got the stuff?"

"Yeah."

"Well, maybe you can tell me what it is," Barney griped.

"See, you just don't destroy enough cars, otherwise you'd know."

"Funny. So spill."

"It's a parts list for cars or for *a* car; I can't tell which. I also can't tell you what kind of car or truck or pickup it might be, and I'm stumped as to the significance of it. Maybe it's a Brinks truck filled with money. Did you check out the paper, you know, for maybe a hidden message or something. Hiding something on these innocuous sheets would be a perfect dodge."

"Naw, I looked. There's no watermark or anything else I could find. I tried the lemon-juice test. Nothing there. I don't have the equipment to do a color spectrum test. Maybe you should hand it off to the cops."

"Not yet. It's better that they think we're completely in the dark—which isn't too far from the truth."

"Okay," returned Barney. "So, what do we do?"

Taylor was silent for a second.

"Taylor? You still there?"

"Yeah, yeah. Listen. This is asking a lot, Barn. I don't know if I should..."

"I've been supporting you since forever. What's the difference now?"

"Thanks Barn. Okay, here's the deal. Can you make a hard copy of these pages?"

"No problem."

"Okay. Then make the copies, and put the originals in the safe."

"Got it."

"Good. Then I want you to take the copies to Ricky Villereal's repair shop on Santa Monica."

"Ricky's?"

"He repairs all my cars after I destroy them. You can find his address online. Anyway, take the pages to him and tell him I need to know what he makes out of this list. He deals in this stuff every day. Leave the copies if he needs them. Just make sure he knows that they're important and could be dangerous. He must keep them strictly confidential. I'll reimburse him when I get back."

"All right. Will do."

"Thanks Barn."

"My pleasure. By the way, when you gettin' back?"

"Hopefully in just a couple of days."

"You want me to call Abby?"

"Already took care of it. And Barn..."

"Yeah?"

"Play this one close to the vest. Like I said, three people have been murdered because of this thing. I don't want my best friend to join them."

"Got'cha!"

With that, Taylor hung up.

CHAPTER 9

The final destination for the passengers on the *Flying Cloud* was Santorini. It was a weird semi-circle shaped island. It wasn't always like that, of course. Once it was a complete island called Thera. The only problem with Thera was that it had a big honking volcano plunk in the middle of it, and one day as these things are wont to do, it went "Kaboom." There are atolls all over the world where something similar has happened. It's just that this happened in historical times, and a lot of lore built up around the event.

Because much of the island sank, to this day lots of people believe Thera was the legendary Atlantis. Even if that's too whimsically hypothetical, what is fact is that its destruction marked the end of the Minoan civilization. Others have attempted to link the cataclysmic explosion to the events in Egypt when the Hebrews challenged Pharaoh and there ensued the ten plagues that included results which characteristically might happen after a volcanic eruption and pyroclastic blast. Whatever the truth of the matter, the remainder of Thera's caldera is now called Santorini. It sits in the sea fronted by one half of a parens with the ubiquitous Greek-style whitewashed houses along the top of the cliffs of the island above where ships drop anchor. Unknown to many, however, is that there is a mound building beneath the sea in the same spot where the original volcano stood, and one day it will explode just as it did some 3600 years ago.

Taylor had spent a restless night. There were no messages from anyone, and he was on pins and needles about what Ricky Villereal could tell him. To hell with all those snobby computer geeks who thought everything in the world turned on their keystrokes, it was guys like Ricky, real men, whom he'd trust more to get the goods. Trouble is, even with Ricky, he'd have to cool his heels and wait for information, so it was back to his original job at least until he got a ring from Barney. Fortunately, Santorini was the last stop the fam would make before the trip back to Barcelona.

While other cruise lines made Malta the final stop, this cruise would sew up everything with an uninterrupted sail back to the original port of Barcelona in one go.

Taylor was up at six as usual although he hadn't really slept much the previous night. He knew he'd pay for it later. Meanwhile, he was back in security mode and down at the buffet at his usual time. Once again he spotted Mandy's friends Anna and Casey. He smiled and waved to the both of them. They smiled and waved back. The world was still in its proper orbit.

Cassandra had already informed everybody that the island wasn't the kind of place the kids could negotiate very easily. Like Mykonos, they would mostly be walking as her friend Joy had warned her. For that reason, the kids would stay on board again and enjoy the kid attractions even if they'd enjoyed them before. Mandy assured her that at the very least the ship's entertainment schedule showed there would be movies that the kids hadn't yet seen. And, of course, they never got tired of the pool or the water slides. Those alone could take up most of the day.

As usual, Alan had prearranged for a limo to pick them up next to the parked busses. The new chauffeur/guide was Georgios. As per usual, he'd drive them around the island and take them to the best spots for lunch, shopping, or anything else they wished to do. For Cassandra, of course, that meant shopping. Georgios also provided a continuous line of patter about the history and topography of the island together with descriptions of the life of the people and the vineyards that lined some of the barren hills. There were even wine-tasting rooms that Cassandra's friend Joy Engdahl had told her were an absolute must to visit.

Thus, after taking the grand tour of the island by car, Georgios led three tourist through the main town, Fira Village, with many of its shops sporting the now familiar Greek kitsch. Surprisingly, Cassandra didn't purchase very much, probably because she already had picked up a lot of the same stuff at Athens and Mykonos except for the glass paper weight with some of Thera's volcanic rock frozen inside which she bought and dropped into her purse.

After the previous restful day they had had on the beach at Mykonos, they decided to take a long lunch at a clifftop restaurant where they could look out over the ocean and see their ship that didn't look so imposing from this vantage point. Alan and Cass both had Ouzo. After couple of glasses of the stuff, Alan ordered a bottle of Sans Rival from which they drank at their leisure. Alan commented that it had a noticeable licorice flavor, but Cassandra said the flavor reminded her of her Oma's Pfeffernüsse, the gingerbread cookies that her grandma used to bake for the family when she was a kid. Taylor drank a couple of Cokes. Along with the Ouzo, Alan had shrimp—with the heads still attached—and Cassandra had the Calamari. All three had salads with feta cheese and plenty of limp garden greens, olives, and other unidentifiable peppers all drenched in a vinegarette dressing. Cassandra liked it so much she said she'd make it at home. Alan wasn't enthusiastic, and Taylor was indifferent. He preferred the baby iceberg wedge salad with blue cheese dressing that he always got at Musso and Frank.

After a day of playing tourist and of eating and drinking the local fare, they all decided that it was time to pack it in and get back to the ship. As it turned out, they found once again that you actually had to work to have fun.

Their speedboat beat the shuttles back to the ship. They swiped in their IDs and headed for their staterooms. Since it was only after four in the afternoon, Alan asked Taylor to wait a half hour so that he and Cass could freshen up before going down to get the kids. Taylor was happy to comply since he was eager to check his phone for messages.

In fact, his phone was loaded. First was Abby who reported that she'd reached her parents' place, and while they were surprised by her visit, she was welcomed and safe. She'd wait for his call.

Palfrey was next in line. He reported that while they were checking their passenger manifest, they discovered that Mr. Bey apparently had left the ship at Piraeus and had not checked back in when they left. "After you mentioned him in connection with the tennis shoes, I thought you ought to know, sir," he said. Taylor immediately punched in a number.

"Palfrey. Taylor here," he said. "So Ardie Bey is missing you say?"

"Seems to be the case," he replied.

"What about his wife and daughter?"

"Excuse me, sir?"

"His wife and daughter. What happened to them?" Taylor asked, a little perturbed.

"But sir," Palfrey replied evenly. "Mr. Bey was alone on this trip. He had one of our small staterooms on a lower deck with a twin bed. There *was* no wife or daughter."

Taylor was speechless for a second.

"I don't understand. I saw him with a woman and a child. He said he had a wife and daughter."

"Well, it seems the fellow was stringing you along, sir. We have no record of any such thing."

Taylor nodded to himself. "Uh, yeah, Palfrey. Thanks," he returned absently.

"Quite all right, sir. Always happy to help," the Chief Officer replied and rang off.

Taylor tapped his index finger on the table top as he attempted to think through this turn of events. Ardie lied—flat out lied. And he wore Vans. Was he the assailant? It was possible and now even seemed more than probable. And he never got back on the ship when it was anchored at Piraeus. If he knew why, it could be important, maybe for himself, but more importantly, maybe for Alan.

The next call was from Mott. It was short and sweet. "We found your missing guy—Millner," was all he said and then hung up.

Taylor feverishly punched in Mott's number, but all he got was the outgoing message. Jesus, he'd forgotten! It was 2 a.m. back in L.A. He'd have to wait to talk to him. However, the last name on the list wouldn't present that problem—Barney. Barney didn't ever go to bed before 4 a.m. And his message said he had something from Ricky. He punched in the number.

"Barney's," answered the familiar voice.

"It's me. You said you had something from Ricky."

"Well, it's not much, but it's something."

"Okay."

"Well, seems you were right; it is a car parts list. He says that judging from the parts he sees, it looks to be an older sports car—maybe something on the order of an older Ferrari California. He says a '52 through '56 Ferrari 290 MM in prime condition can go for as much as $23 million bucks or thereabouts."

"And that's what we have here?"

"He's not sure of the make, model, or year, but from the manifest he says these are old car parts going back to the fifties or sixties; so, we're probably talking about some sort of classic car."

"$23 million bucks is an adequate reason for a murder; but I wonder..."

"Wonder what?"

"Not sure yet. Anyway, thanks, Barn; ya might have saved my life again."

"What else is new."

Taylor chuckled. "I'll keep you posted. Go get some sleep, and if you have a chance, tell Ricky I'll thank him personally when I get back."

"I hear ya," returned Barney and rang off.

Taylor sat for a second and stared at the wall thinking. The car thing would certainly explain the murder of Ross and Tabby. It would even explain the attacks on him if they weren't about Alan and his problem. But he still didn't have enough information to come to any conclusions. Besides, it was time to get the kids and go to dinner.

When he buzzed, he was surprised to find that Mandy and the kids had already come back to their stateroom and cleaned up for dinner. They'd had a long day and spent much of it in the pool as they wanted to. This tired them out, so Mandy brought them back early, and they took a little nap. They were hungry and actually ready for dinner.

Taylor escorted Alan and his brood to the dining room where they sat as usual at their reserved table. Steak and prime rib were on the menu for the evening, after which the parents promised that the kids could select whatever they wanted from the dessert buffet which was something to see. They had six different kinds of torts covered in green, peach and raspberry colored fondant. There was New York cheesecake, a luscious mile-high chocolate cake, delectable rum babas, an Italian rum cake, and several flavors of ice cream including coffee flavor. After the sumptuous dinner of rare beef, lyonnaise potatoes, and sauteed asparagus, the dessert felt like overkill, but it was difficult to refuse. For Taylor, the rum cake went down just fine with a nice latte.

After the meal, the family decided to take in a movie in the Magic Theater. It was an old Shaggy-Dog comedy from the sixties that the parents and kids could both enjoy. Taylor saw to it that Alan was seated strategically where he'd be safest, and he waited just outside the theater at a coffee bar with Mandy who was happy to have the parents handle the kids at least for a while.

He ordered a latte, and she ordered her English breakfast tea with cream. It was a balmy and seductive night. Under other circumstances it might even have been somewhat romantic. But that wasn't happening.

"So, how'd it go with the kids today?" he asked.

She looked up at him from under her eyebrows. "You must be joking."

"No. Just wondering."

She sighed. "Well, about the same as all the other days. It's not that the kids wear me out, I love them as though they were my own. But when you're trapped together with about a hundred of them and they're all shouting, laughing, and crying out for two hours straight, it kind of takes it out of you."

"I can imagine," returned Taylor.

"How was Santorini?" she asked out of nowhere.

"Pretty much like Mykonos. Not the bountiful and verdant fields of Elysium you might imagine from *The Iliad* and *The Odyssey* but merely dirt, dry scrub brush, heat, and a mostly desolate landscape sometimes with piles of ancient stones where temples once stood, sometimes not."

"But not the towns certainly."

"No, you're right. They are a maze of little lanes and cramped allées with stores hawking kitschy tchotchkes that people buy to take home and eventually stick into a cardboard box in the garage."

"Wow, you're kind of cynical, aren't you," she observed.

"Just realistic. You have no idea how crass a world it is out there," he returned.

"That doesn't sound like something a math teacher from Conniston Public Middle School in Palm Beach Florida would say."

"Ah, you remembered. But you haven't been to Florida."

"Then, I take it you're saying I didn't actually miss too much at Mykonos and Santorini."

"I wouldn't say that. You certainly missed the Ouzo."

"Ouzo?"

"Greek booze. Flavored like licorice or Pfeffernüsse, well, depending on whom you ask."

Mandy chuckled. "I'm not much for alcohol although I might have a little glass of wine now and again."

"Tell you what, I'll treat you to Sangria when we get back to Barcelona."

Mandy smiled broadly. "That's a date. Think we can see the city together when we get there?"

"Maybe; that is, if I survive the next couple of days of the trip," he put in, thinking that if the assassins hadn't been successful before, they only had a little time left to score.

"Oh," she returned teasingly without catching his meaning, "it won't be that bad. And we'll be back sooner than you can imagine."

"Um. Yeah, I know that," he said.

They finished their drinks and took a turn around the promenade. Taylor took furtive looks at his phone to see if Alan had buzzed him while they walked. By the time they got back, the movie was over, and the crowd was exiting the theater, Taylor stood near the door where he could keep an eye on Alan who followed his directions and waited for everyone to leave before he did. Cassandra and the kids always chafed at this delay, but Alan, on Taylor's recommendation, explained that he just didn't like contending with the crowds.

As per their routine, Taylor accompanied everyone to their staterooms, and then he went to his own. Once inside he checked his phone for messages and found a slew of them. The first on the list was from Marge for him to call. He checked his watch. It was about eight o'clock in the morning. Marge would be in. He punched in the number.

"Pierce Investigations," Marge answered.

"It's me. I got your message."

"Ah. Bubbie," she said, "I was finally able to get back to your stuff. Jesus, what a meshugas! I checked out your verkackte business, this Sunshine Collectibles LLC that Ross and Millner owned. Turns out it they didn't really own it; they just ran it."

"So, who owned it?"

"Uh... it was... ah, here it is," she said as she paged through her notes. "Yeah, turns out the company is a subsidiary of Universal Imports International which was a subsidiary of Worldwide Commodities which was..."

"Jesus! How far down the rabbit hole does this thing go?"

"That was what was so tough to find out. There are at least a half dozen alias companies."

"So, what's the primary holder?"

"Seems to be an outfit called Global Capital Investments. They're headquartered right here in L.A. in Century City."

"Got the name of the head honcho?"

"Brick wall. That's as far as I could get. But what I can tell you is that this company is a big deal with offices in Paris, London, Madrid, Athens, Buenos Aires, Tokyo, and Hong Kong."

"Good work, Marge" he returned enthusiastically. I owe you a box of doughnuts."

"Don't you dare!" she shot back. "I've lost three pounds since you've been gone."

Taylor chuckled. "Okay, I'll make it a nice bag of keto approved pitted dried prunes," he said and rang off.

Surprisingly, the second call was from Harry. He punched in his number.

"Taylor? That you?" he asked.

"Yeah," he replied.

"Well, what the hell did you just say to Marge? She called you a couple of names I can't even repeat," he said.

"She'll get over it," he replied. "So what did you call about?"

"Y'know, I guess it's comforting to realize that even half a world away, you still come off like an ass. Anyway , how's the job. You haven't reported," he said, suddenly changing the topic.

"Ya mean Alan? Heck, Alan's doing just peachy. I'm the one that's bushed watching over him every nanosecond of the day," Taylor replied.

"Well, that's good because you can tell him that the heat's off."

"Huh?"

"You heard me. The Feds had a sit down with the principals, and everything was ironed out. They don't need Wells or anything he knows, might know, or thinks he knows. It's all inert information and can't hurt anyone because they pleaded to a lesser charge and paid a relatively small fine which was the cheapest way to get out of the whole thing. Wells has been embraced, forgiven, and relieved of duty. He's been put out to pasture, separated from their businesses, and given a huge payout. And that's it. Wells can come home and live a wonderful retirement in Brentwood, go golfing every day, and eat latkes at Jerry's Deli to his heart's content for as long as he likes."

Taylor sat, stunned. "No kiddin'?"

"No kiddin'. He's probably gotten the memo already, but you can tell him for me anyway. And as of now, you're off the hook, buddy. Enjoy the rest of the trip then come back home and do some real work."

"Right!" scoffed Taylor. "I'll call you when I'm back."

He sat back in his chair and took a breath. Wow, what a surprise, he thought. He could wait until morning to tell Alan, but he was pretty sure he'd like to hear about this right now. It would be quite a relief to him. He picked up his phone and punched in Alan's number.

"Alan..." he began but was cut off.

"Taylor, I got it!" he said excitedly. "Oh, man. What a relief!"

"Congratulations!' replied Taylor. "Glad it worked out for you. Now get a good night's sleep. See you in the morning."

"Absolutely," returned Alan. "You're off the clock. Show up when you like. I'm sure you can use the rest. And Taylor..."

"Yeah?"

"Thanks, man. Thanks for everything. You need anything—anything at all—you just ask."

Alan hung up and Taylor nodded to himself. Alan was a nice guy, a good father, and uncomplaining no matter what Taylor asked of him. He deserved a win in this deal. It was nice to see that at least sometimes the good guys come out on top.

Taylor was contemplating hitting the sack when he remembered that there was one more message to read. It was Mott who asked him to call him back. A couple of keys punched in, and there he was.

"Taylor, you got my message."

"Just that you called."

"Ah. Well, we finally found that guy."

"Yeah. Millner. You said that."

"Yeah, Martin Millner. Right."

"But where?"

"We had to go through the Feds. It took a lot of time and the search was difficult, but they got him through the TSA."

"He was taking a flight?"

"Yeah, he had to use his passport of course. They're electronically logged in at the airports. Apparently, he'd previously gone through the security screening and they'd checked out his background and had his fingerprints taken. Part of the problem for us is that he's just a regular guy. He'd had a couple of civil suits, but otherwise he was a solid citizen as far as we know who wasn't wanted for anything illegal or criminal. I mean, he hasn't broken any laws or anything. He never even got a parking ticket. That's why running his name and making sure he was the same guy from North Carolina and Florida was so difficult."

"Okay, I get it," he returned, a bit overwhelmed by the lengthy explanation.

"Well, it took us a lot of work to find this guy..."

"I appreciate that."

"And I just wanted you to know."

"Thank you Lieutenant Mott and your staff..."

"Rodriguez."

"Thank you and Sergeant Rodriguez! Okay?"

"Okay."

"Now, may we cut to the chase?" asked Taylor with a little snarky emphasis.

"Sure. We were right. He *was* in L.A. Then we clocked him in at LAX yesterday afternoon. He got on a flight heading for Greece," he reported.

"Greece?"

"Athens, apparently."

Taylor's eyes darted back and forth for a second.

Oh, my God, he thought. Of course Athens. That's where Ross was going. That's where Tabby was going. Why hadn't he seen it before?

"Uh... thanks, thanks. I'll get back to you," he said hurriedly and rang off. Then he punched in a number.

"Pierce Investigations," answered she of the crimson lips and hair color.

"It's me again," he said almost sheepishly.

"You gotta lot of nerve intimating that I'm an old fart who needs..."

"It's about Brooke Cameron's murder."

"Oh," she said more coolly. "What is it?"

"That company that has connections in Greece..."

"Athens."

"Right. Athens. Do you happen to have an address?"

"Hang on," she said. "Lemme check my stuff."

Marge put down the phone. He could hear her going through papers. It seemed to take forever. Then she picked up again.

"Yeah, I got it. Right here."

"And?"

"Uh, there are two addresses."

"Both in Athens?"

"Yeah, but one is downtown—I'll bet that's the headquarters. The other one is in a place called Aspropyrgos. A business address for Trans-Mediterranean Import/Exports on Megaridos Street wherever in the hell that is," she stated.

"Great. Gimme both addresses," he said. "By the way, do you like Ouzo?"

Taylor scribbled down the information and thanked Marge again—properly this time. She wished him well, especially if he was taking steps to nail the bastard who killed Brooke Cameron. He promised he'd do his best.

He next phoned Alan again who was just about to hit the sack.

"Alan," he said. "You remember you told me that all I had to do was ask if I needed anything?"

"Yeah," the man replied.

Ten minutes later Taylor was on the bridge with Palfrey, Captain Drake, and Dr. Wyndham-Smythe.

"You need what?" inquired the good doctor with an elongated breathy "ah" sound in the middle of "what."

"A helicopter. You can get one can't you?"

"But, Mr. Taylor..."

"It's the murderer. I'm sure I know where he's going. If I can get there now, I may be able to catch him. But I need a helicopter to get to Athens, and I need the help of the police. Once I get there, I've already got transportation 'laid on,' as you fellows say."

"You're certain about this?" asked Captain Drake.

"As certain as you can be about anything," he replied. "But listen, this is what I've got. You be the judge."

Taylor then went on to explain his problem with Ardeth Bey, the fact that he wore Vans, the fact that he lied about having a family, and the fact that he got off the ship at Athens. Then he told them of Tabby's family, how her sister Brooke and her fiancé Bob were murdered, and that Bob and Tabby coincidentally were also heading for Athens. To this he also revealed that he was told by the police that Martin Millner—the other individual involved in a business that dealt in pricey collectibles, antiques, and stuff had been in L.A. but coincidentally had just taken a plane to—where? To Athens. Was he the one who killed Brooke Cameron? Maybe; maybe not. However, he was certainly involved somehow. Finally, Taylor explained about the document that Brooke Cameron apparently secreted to Taylor's office and which held the probable reason she and the others were killed. It was some rare object—probably an old classic car that was worth some twenty-odd million dollars. She may have thought giving him the document was some sort of insurance policy. Unfortunately for her, it wasn't.

The other men almost had to catch their breath at the recitation. All of these clues coming together looked like far more than coincidence. They asked what his plan was and what he had in mind. He told them about the address in Athens that his operative in L.A. had dug up. One was an office in the downtown area. Probably the headquarters for Global Capital Investments. Meanwhile, their warehouse was located in Aspropyrgos, and he had the business address for Trans-Mediterranean Import/Exports on Megaridos Street which was probably where Millner and Bey were headed.

"Well, gentlemen?" said Captain Drake as he looked at Palfrey and the doctor. "I think you can appreciate what a difficult decision this is."

"Absolutely, sir. But let me just say that I have grown to have a good deal of respect for Mr. Taylor."

"Here, here," seconded Palfrey.

Drake sighed. "Our sailing line has never had a murder of the kind we had left unexplained, Mr. Taylor. Plus, I must tell you that I took it as a personal failing that Miss Young, who put such great faith in us, was let down in the most despicable way. Because of all that..." he said as he nodded to himself, "we're going to support you fully in this instance."

The ship had a helicopter landing pad at the very front of the ship with a big "H" marked in the middle of a circle, It's where Leonardo DiCaprio held Kate Winslet on the bow of the Titanic and shouted that he was "the King of the World." Not so today.

Taylor left a message for Alan that thanked him for his help and with that got onto the helicopter. The bird flew out over the Mediterranean which gave Taylor an unparalleled view of the waters and what was beneath them.

It was afternoon before the helicopter reached the air field. The pilot said that he'd made the contacts that Taylor had requested, and that he had standing orders to wait for Taylor to return for the flight back to the ship.

As Taylor stepped off the copter, a limo pulled up, and a man jumped out of the driver's seat.

"Dimitrios! Good to see you," said Taylor.

"You too, Mr. Taylor. Mr. Wells has told me to take you anywhere you wish to go."

Taylor pulled a piece of paper from his pocket.

"You know this place?" he asked.

"Aspropyrgos? Of course. It's an industrial area."

Taylor smiled. "Just as I thought. Take me there. But when we get there, park a little away from the facility. This will take some stealth. By the way, did you bring it?" he asked.

"Yes, sir, here," replied Dimitrios as he handed something to Taylor. "A brand new Beretta APX A1."

"Loaded?" asked Taylor as he checked the magazine.

"Of course," Dimitrios replied.

"Good. Then let's get going," he said.

The drive to the destination took over an hour. The Athens International Airport where he landed was clear across town not far from Vravrona Beach on the eastern coast. Aspropyrgos was far to the west which required Dimitrios to take all sorts of highways and byways.

Taylor sat quietly in the back of the limo working out his plan while he drank a Coke from the car's fridge. Although he'd given the name of the company and the headquarter's address to Captain Drake to relay to the authorities, he didn't tell him about the place they were actually headed—a warehouse in the light industry area of town on Megaridos Street to the east of Agiou Georgiou. That's where his intuition indicated the others would be.

It was dark when they arrived. Taylor had Dimitrios cut the headlights and drive slowly past the warehouse where the lighted side of the building read "Trans-Mediterranean Import/Exports." They proceeded down the road for another fifty yards and Taylor had Dimitrios park on the right side of the road on the dirt shoulder underneath a small stand of Salt Cedar trees. He turned the car off. Taylor exited the car and went to the driver's window.

"Okay," he said as he handed Dimitrios another piece of paper. "I want you to wait five minutes and then call this number. This is the police. Tell them where we are and to come running. Tell them to use the GPS on your phone. Whatever, but get them here."

"Yes, sir," replied the driver.

"Good man. All right," he said as he checked the Beretta and then stuck it under his belt on the left side, "here we go."

Taylor jogged off to the warehouse that they'd just passed. There were a couple of old cars and pickup trucks parked in front of an eight foot tall metal-bar fence. He followed the fence to a gate that, surprisingly, was unlocked. He opened it gingerly as the thing creaked a little on its rusted hinges. He stopped, but there was no movement, no sound. He headed for the warehouse.

The building looked old, like a huge, thirty-foot high Quonset hut with a rounded roof and sides made of corrugated steel. The long side of the building was solid with no door. The front, however, had a huge door on the front and next to it a regular-sized passage door with a dirty glass pane on the upper part. Taylor could see a light through the glass. He went to open the door and again found that it was already ajar. He opened it and entered as quietly as he could.

The place was filled with rows of boxes stacked to the ceiling and looked like the warehouse at the end of *Raiders of the Lost Ark*. He could hear talking apparently coming from the far corner of the place. He increased his speed through the rows and rows until the light became brighter and the talking louder.

"No!" No!" he heard someone yell as he raced to the spot in time to see the backlit form of a man as he took a swipe at another with a large knife.

"Freeze!" yelled Taylor as he leveled the Beretta at the man with the knife.

"Bang!" He fired the gun once into the ceiling.

"Drop your weapon and hit the pavement," he yelled as he moved towards the figure.

The guy dropped the knife and hit the floor at once.

The man he'd injured who was on the ground bleeding groaned. "My shoulder. My shoulder," the man cried.

"S'okay. The police will be here in a second," Taylor promised. "Just stay cool. And as for you, Ardie..." he said as he stood before the prone figure.

But as the man raised his face to look at Taylor, he realized that it wasn't Ardie.

"Hi, mate," said the man in a cockney accent.

"Mike? What in the hell..."

Sure enough. It was the guy he'd been seeing almost daily at the coffee bar for the better part of the trip. Next to him lay a knife that looked very much like the one they pulled out of his headboard.

"You! You're the one who attacked me and murdered Tabby Young."

"Now, why would I do that?" returned Mike innocently.

"How 'bout because you're a paid killer. Man, I've got to hand it to you. I don't get fooled very often, but you were perfect. I never would have guessed."

"You're just making it all up."

"Naw. It was you in my room. You with the knife—just like that one on the floor. And you slaughtered Tabitha Young with it."

"Wasn't me. I'm just a..."

"Right. Tell it to the cops. Now stand up and grab the wall."

Mike stood up and made like he was going to do as told; however, instead he turned and whipped his leg around, thus kicking the gun out of Taylor's hand so that it skidded on the floor. Taylor made for the gun, but Mike was on him in a second. Taylor responded with a couple of karate chops and a leg kick, but Mike took it all. Then, seeing the gun, he dove for it. Taylor saw that he and the gun were out of reach, so he dove for the knife. Mike grabbed the gun and leveled it at Taylor. But Taylor grabbed the knife and deftly threw it as hard as he could at Mike.

The force of the blow hit Mike's chest with a loud "crack" as the serrated blade penetrated through the man's sternum and through his heart.

"Bang! Bang!" went the gun as Mike managed to get off a couple of wild shots. Then he collapsed back onto the floor, dead.

"Taylor," he then heard someone running behind him and looked up to see Ardie Bey.

"Oh, great! What now?" he quipped as he still lay prone on the floor half expecting to get shot or something.

"Good work! We've been after these characters for quite a while."

"Excuse me. We?" he said incredulously.

"INTERPOL, Mr. Taylor. This is part of a gang of thieves who deal in stolen artifacts like that one over there," he said as he pointed at what was clearly an automobile that was covered. He walked to the injured man on the floor.

"Well, Mr. Millner, do you think you're ready to tell us everything now, or would you be more comfortable as an accessory to murder?"

"I'll talk. I'll talk. Just get me some help for my shoulder."

"Ambulance and travel back to the hospital and then to the police already laid on," replied Ardie.

He walked to the car and put his hand on the front fender. "All that murder; all that death just for this," he said.

"Yeah, I don't get it either," put in Taylor as he got to his feet. Three people dead over a Ferrari?"

Ardie laughed. "A Ferrari? No, no my friend. A Ferrari—even one of the rarest in mint condition would probably only have brought in maybe twenty to twenty-five million. But this car is special. It would easily bring in, what, Millner?"

"Fifty million," the man mumbled.

"What!" exclaimed Taylor. A lousy car for fifty million dollars?"

"Not just *any* car, Taylor. This one," he explained as he grabbed the car cover and with one stroke tore it off onto the floor.

And there it was.

A silver beauty that looked like it just came off of the showroom floor. Sleek, low, chromed wire wheels, quick-change knockoffs. Sure, he'd seen it before; who hadn't?

"This is the one and only. The original," explained Ardie. "Chassis identification number DP216/1."

"Oh, man. *That's* what that number was!"

"Yes," confirmed Ardie. "And I have to tell you, Taylor. Without you, we never would have caught up with the gang or finally found the original James Bond Aston Martin DB5 that was used in *Goldfinger.* You have my thanks, the thanks of the actual owner, and the thanks of INTERPOL."

CHAPTER 10

"And the whole thing focused on this car, James Bond's 1963 DB5," Taylor was just explaining.

"No!" exclaimed Dr. Guy Wyndham-Smythe. "Why, that's unbelievable," he said as Captain Drake and Palfrey stood with him on the bridge of the *Flying Cloud* listening to Taylor's narrative.

"Let me tell it to you the way I got it from Agent Bey," continued Taylor.

"This was the original 1963 Aston Martin DB 5 that was used in *Goldfinger* and *Thunderball*. After the second film was finished, the car was returned to the Aston Martin factory where it was stripped of all those neat gadgets that they used in the films—you know, the machine guns, oil spray, smoke screen, all that stuff. I assume they did that probably because it legally could not be sold as is, and it was being sold to a collector. However, after the sale, that owner put all the gadgets back on and then re-sold it to another guy who lived out West who owned it for about fifteen years."

"By out West, I take it you mean it went to America?" put in Palfrey.

"Yes. The new owner lived in Utah. Then around 1986 he put it up for auction, and it was purchased by a Florida Real Estate magnate for the then huge sum of $250,000 dollars. Can you imagine! Anyway, for a decade the car was displayed at car shows, Bond extravaganzas, and other such events. All that lasted until 1997 when the DB5 was mysteriously stolen from a guarded and secured hangar at the airport in Boca Raton, never to be seen again."

"Gone all those years, and no one had a clue?" asked the doctor.

"Not a clue. But the owner was reimbursed to the tune of about four million dollars, just to show how the car's value had improved. However, as I said, just what happened to the automobile and where it was located during all those years up to today is still something of a mystery. In fact, in the end there was an anonymous tip, and the people who held it may just have thought it was too hot a property to hang onto. Or, they may never have known that it was stolen property in the first place but didn't want to be involved."

"That's amazing," said Palfrey.

"Anyway, this is where *our* story picks up—*mine* anyway. Apparently, our boys—Bob Ross and Martin Millner—got wind of the car and its location and according to Millner were able to wangle a deal involving trades for some expensive Renaissance and modern art works. That's how they gained control over the car. More importantly, Millner told us that they had a deal with one guy who was willing to pay around $25 million dollars for it. The group would have been satisfied with that cut, but then another buyer, whom I'll call Mr. Big, popped up who said he actually would double that price to $50 million and would not stop at absolutely anything to get it. Mr. Big laid out a down payment and thought it was a done deal. But the seeming ease with which the group managed to get the price doubled got Ross, Millner and the sisters, Brooke and Tabitha, to thinking. Stupidly, they got greedy and went back to the first buyer and also to others to see if they could get an even better price and a resultant bigger cut. What they didn't know was that Mr. Big wasn't someone you could cross or mess with, and when he heard about what they were doing, he sent out his goons to deal with these people."

"And who was that?" interjected Palfrey.

"That was our friend and your employee, Mike the barista—or Philip Michael Matsen formerly of Brixton in London. He purposely murdered Brooke Cameron in such a hideous fashion just to scare the hell out of her compatriots. Matsen found out about Ross and Tabitha and the cruise from Brooke Cameron and managed to work his way into a job on your ship not just to get Ross and Tabitha but also to get *me*."

"To get you? But why?" queried Wyndham-Smythe.

"And Ross was murdered on the plane even before he got here," interjected Captain Drake. "How?"

"Yes," replied Taylor, addressing the captain, "I'm not quite sure precisely how he pulled off Ross' murder, but I'm assuming he had a compatriot on the plane."

"Any idea who that might be?" asked the captain.

"My guess is that everyone was supposed to meet in Athens. Since we didn't catch them there, they must have gotten wind of the operation and gotten away."

"But please go on with your story," urged Palfrey.

"All right. Like I said, they were also after me. Why? Well, it's like this. See, I took a job with Brooke Cameron in L.A. about a domestic dispute with her husband that had nothing at all to do with the Aston Martin situation. But

Brooke stupidly became involved with Ross and Millner because she thought that with her cut of the money, she could become truly independent from her husband, Anson Cameron. I'll bet her sister talked her into it. Even so, she was still a little skittish about the deal and apparently sent me papers at our office concerning the Aston Martin. My guess is that she thought it would be some sort of insurance policy. Problem for her was, it wasn't, and she was murdered anyway. Apparently, before she was knocked off, she also must have mentioned me to Bob Ross who made it a point to connect with me at the airport on the way to Barcelona. Anyway, the result of her action from the bad guys' perspective was that Matsen and Mr. Big were certain that I was in on Ross', Millner's, and Tabitha's double dealing. As a result, my firm's office and my own home were ransacked. And that's also why I was attacked on the ship. They followed me."

"So, who was this Mr. Big and the person who murdered Ross?" asked the doctor.

Taylor shook his head. "No idea. However, I imagine Mr. Big's hopping mad that he lost the car along with his down payment. As for the person who got Ross, I have a couple of ideas and am having our secretary check some records as is Agent Bey. But honestly, we'll probably never know their identities. In my business, sometimes that's just part of the game."

"Ra-ther," remarked the doctor in his inimitable inflection.

Captain Drake stretched out his arm and straightened one sleeve and then the other. "Well, gentlemen, we've got a ship to run and a cruise to finish," he said. "I suggest we return to our stations and make sure everything is shipshape. Mr. Taylor, thank you for your help. I wish you a more relaxing rest of the cruise," he concluded.

"Thank you, Captain Drake. As much as I hate travel over water, you have made this a most enjoyable trip."

The men shook hands all around, and Taylor left the bridge.

It was a bright, sunny day. Taylor went down to deck 12 and sat himself at the coffee bar.

"A latte, Tommy," he said to the barista.

"Comin' right up, Mr. Taylor," the man responded.

Taylor sat back and looked around at the humanity that was walking all around the deck and stopping by the other kiosks that had cold drinks, ice cream bars and sundaes, fresh fruit, and a number of other goodies. All you had to do was ask for whatever you wanted. He sipped thoughtfully at his coffee thinking about the creeps that got away from him when just then his phone went off. He paged through his messages and smiled a little to himself as he turned off his phone and put it into his pocket.

"Can anyone get a drink around this place?" suddenly rang a familiar voice.

"Tommy," said Taylor unprompted, "I think the lady will have an English Breakfast tea with cream..."

"And sugar," interjected Mandy.

She sat down next to him and put her tea together.

"Where were you yesterday afternoon and evening?" she asked.

"Had some business to take care of."

"On this boat?"

"Ship," he corrected.

"Right. But on this ship? Really?" she challenged.

"You'd be surprised at all the things that go on around here. Tommy, tell her."

"Oh, yeah, lots of stuff," replied the barista tongue in cheek.

"Um," she grunted unconvinced. "Anyway, we still have a few more days until we get back to Barcelona."

"So where are Alan and Cassandra?"

"He's taken the kids on the rides and entertainments on board. Mrs. Wells went to the fitness center to use the elliptical."

"Sounds healthy. And you?"

"They gave me time off. Seems that Mr. Wells got some good news that he wanted to celebrate by spending time with the children. So, I can do pretty much what I want."

"And what would that be?" he asked.

Mandy Bannon smiled at Taylor in a way that said a lot more than words. "Y'know, I was just thinking that..."

"Ah, Mr. Taylor," someone suddenly interrupted.

Taylor turned to see the doctor step up to the kiosk.

"So this is where you spend your time, is it?" he said.

"Uh... Doctor Guy Wyndham-Smythe, may I introduce you to Miss Amanda Bannon, M.A. and working on a Ph.D."

The doctor shook Mandy's hand and smiled at her with a slightly rakish grin. "Pleased to meet you. I say, are you good friends with this chap?" he asked, indicating Taylor.

"We've gotten to know each other fairly well on this trip, I'd say."

"Splendid," returned the doctor. "You know, I was just going to bend his ear about the..."

"Doctor," interrupted Taylor who was afraid the man was going to blow his cover, "could you give me a second?" he asked.

"Well, I suppose I..." Wyndham-Smythe was just saying when there was suddenly a horrible screaming from a woman who was running at full tilt towards the three.

She had her right hand extended straight out and was aiming for Taylor with a rabid, wild look on her face as she screamed for all she was worth.

But when she got within striking distance of Taylor, he suddenly gripped her right wrist and bent her arm back towards her throat. She immediately stopped screaming and gasped horribly. Then she fell onto the deck. She gagged, and her eyes rolled back into her head.

"Doctor. Quick," said Taylor. She just injected herself with Tetrodotoxin," he added as he removed the little bulb syringe from her neck. "You'd better get her to sick bay as quickly as possible. Maybe you can save her?"

The doctor stood for a second in shock as also did Mandy. "Oh, of course, of course" he stammered, coming to himself and then pointed at a couple of bystanders. "You two men, get hold of her and lift her gently. Follow me," he said as they lifted up Mandy's friend Casey and walked as quickly as possible behind the doctor. Taylor watched after them as he took a wad of paper towels and wrapped the syringe in it.

Mandy watched him for a second and then took a step back.

"You wouldn't mind telling me just what the hell is going on here, would you?" she said.

———

"What I can tell you is that she wasn't your friend," Taylor was telling Mandy.

"But Casey was always so happy, so bright and cheery."

"I'm sorry, but it was all an act," he asserted.

"An act? But why?" she asked.

Taylor hesitated to answer for a second. "Because she was a paid assassin. She worked with another assassin right here on the ship. Mike..."

"The barista?" she queried.

He nodded. "They were co-workers and lovers. That's why she came after me and was so crazed when she found out that I had killed him when he attacked me."

"Attacked you?"

"Okay, listen. This a little complicated. See, they were working together in order to knock off some people who were involved in a high-stakes theft. Mike generally preferred to kill with a knife. Casey used a toxin. Between them, they killed three people. She killed a man on the airplane on the way to Barcelona to join this cruise. Then she tried to kill me—twice."

"Twice?"

"Remember the day we were in the caves in Malta?"

"Yes."

"She tried to inject me with one of those syringes when the lights went off in the cave. Luckily, she stuck your bag I was holding instead. I had to wash it off just in case to make sure the toxin was removed from the fabric and couldn't hurt you by just touching it."

"Oh, my God!" exclaimed Mandy as she put her fingers to her mouth in dismay.

"Yeah, I know. It's hard to believe. But that's the truth."

"But I don't understand. What was this all about?" she asked.

"Basically, and not to go into a long-winded explanation, it was about $50 million dollars and the ego of some guy who didn't like being made a loser."

"And what did you have to do with all this; you, a middle-school math teacher from Palm Beach, Florida?"

Taylor smushed his lips together and nodded. It had to come out now whether he wanted it to or not.

"Amanda," he said as he chose his words carefully, "Actually, I'm anything *but* a math teacher."

She nodded. "I thought so," she said. "Something always told me that you just aren't the type."

He smirked. "Well, I'd like to think I could be if it came to that."

"So what were you doing? Are you even Alan's cousin?"

"Not that either. I'm a private eye," he confessed flat out. "I was hired as security for Alan who was being threatened by some folks, and he needed protection."

"So, you're not from Florida at all?"

"Our offices are in L.A. in Hollywood," he responded.

Amanda Bannon shook her head. "Wow, you must have thought I was some dumb bunny," she laughed ruefully. "You really played me. Stupid! Stupid! Stupid!" she said as she knocked her head with her hand.

"Hey!" he said as he took her by the shoulders and faced her. "I was straight about everything else, just not my reason for being here. It was a necessary part of the job if I was going to protect Alan from being hurt or possibly even killed. Beyond that, personally I've been square with you all the way down the line."

"Anything else?"

"I work for an outfit called Pierce Investigations and have for many years. Before that I worked for Uncle Sam on a number of what we call dark projects. A number of these called for physical confrontation, and I've had to eliminate killers like Mike from time to time—defensively, of course."

Mandy nodded understanding.

"And is there... someone else, someone close to you?" she asked finally.

"Yes," he replied at once but didn't expand on that.

"I imagine she's pretty, accomplished, and..."

"Amanda," said Taylor as he looked her in the eye. "You're a really special girl. You're pretty, smart, talented. You've got everything. Don't worry, the future will take care of itself. Knowing you as I've come to, I'll tell you straight out—I can't imagine that there's anyone, anywhere that should take up any of the precious time in your life that can be used for things much more profitably for you socially but above all personally."

Mandy looked up to him. Tears welled up in her eyes.

"But, you'll have to excuse me," he said. I have to get to sick bay to see the doctor, his patient, and Captain Drake."

It turned out that Mandy's friend Casey didn't make it, and they put her in the ship's morgue for disposition once they got to Barcelona. Taylor turned over the syringe so that Wyndham-Smythe could give it to the authorities there. At least they could tie up the loose ends of Ross' murder.

Beyond that, the rest of the cruise was kind of quiet, for him, anyway. Since the pretense of his relationship with Alan wasn't necessary anymore, he didn't spend much time with the family and only saw Mandy at a distance as she tended to the kids. In a couple of days he was off the ship and after the five-hour flight from Florida, was back in L.A. with all its attendant negatives.

"So, look who's back," cracked Marge as Taylor walked through the office door, "our own world traveler."

"Yeah. Harry in yet," he remarked dryly.

Marge frowned. "Hey, what the heck's with you, bubbie? You look like crap. What'd they do to you on that cruise?"

Taylor smiled wearily. "I'm okay. Anyway, I come like the Greeks bearing gifts," he stated as he opened a bag and pulled stuff out like it was a cornucopia.

"These are for you. This is for Harry, and this is for Bernstein," he said as he pointed to each of the tchotchkes. I even have a gift card for Bernstein so he can take mortuary girl to dinner. And for you as well, madame, because you did such a great job for me when you didn't have to, I have a couple of things. First, the box of raspberry jelly doughnuts I promised you..."

"Ah! I love 'em, but I shouldn't eat 'em," she managed to say.

"Second, a bottle of Ouzo," he said as he handed it to her.

"...And third, four gift certificates for a couple of dinner evenings for you and your hubby at Musso and Frank any time you want to have them."

For the first time since he'd known Marge, she couldn't say anything, and she couldn't even close her mouth she was so surprised.

"Hey, maybe I should give you these more often. I didn't realize there actually was a way to stop you in mid speech."

But Marge smiled from ear or ear. "This is the nicest thing anyone has ever done for me, Taylor," she said as sweetly as she was able.

He grinned, but didn't let it get to him. "You earned it. Just don't let it get to your head and get all maudlin all over me. And just wait till I hit you with the next assignment!" he said gruffly.

"Thank you, Taylor," she replied simply with a sweetness in her voice he didn't know she had.

"You're welcome, Marge. Now, is Harry around?"

"Won't be in till late. He's picking up some of the jobs you couldn't do because of the trip."

Taylor sighed. "Okay, tell him I'll be in later. I have to pick up someone at LAX."

Taylor left the office and headed back to his apartment. It had taken him the better part of a day to straighten up the place since Mr. Big's goons had ransacked it. Fortunately, they didn't get anything important. He'd already stashed his gun, computer drives, and all his other valuables in his vault at the bank that was just up the street. And despite his fears, and as Mott confirmed, no one had gone into Abby's place which he checked for himself. Thank God for that.

He locked up his place and went to his parking spot, but instead of getting into his usual ride, he stepped over to the car he kept covered, the car for which he paid extra for a spot to park. Only his Camry was parked next to it. On the other side of the covered car was a wall. He'd take off the cover every couple of weeks and start the thing to make sure nothing had seized up. Why he didn't drive it, he couldn't tell you, but today he felt like it.

He pulled off the cover to reveal the sleek, silver Aston Martin concept car that used to belong to Scott Foster but was given to him by his wife at the end of Foster's murder case. Next to this car, James Bond's DB5 looked fairly dumpy. And although this Aston Martin didn't come with machine guns, oil spray, smoke screen, and all that stuff, when you pushed the gas pedal, the thing took off like a bat outa hell. He looked it over and decided he needed to wax it when he got a chance. Then he got in and cranked it.

The drive to LAX was its usual stupid. He usually got off the freeway at Howard Hughes and took Sepulveda all the way down to the airport where it was easier to drop off people on the upper level. But this time he had to pick up, so he took the Century Boulevard offramp and headed for the airport's lower level where passengers exited each airline. He stopped in front of one of them and maneuvered his car into a spot where he could wait. It only took about five minutes before she appeared.

It'd been a while. He'd almost forgotten how she walked, the cute way she smiled, and how her eyes beamed when she looked up at him like nothing else in the universe existed. In a second Abby was in his arms and sharing a warm, sweet kiss with him. And then another. And then another. Then they broke off, and she went for her suitcase.

"Here, lemme take that," he said as she bent to grab her bag.

"Ooh," she gushed. "You came in the sportscar," she said as she looked up and checked out his ride.

Taylor chuckled as he let her in on the passenger side. Then he got into the driver's side.

"Yeah. I decided to take her out more often," he explained. "It doesn't do to keep such a thing of beauty hidden from the world."

Abby Hart looked him over with practiced nonchalance. "It seems you had quite an adventure on this job, I can tell. As though something unexpected happened to you," she observed.

He chuckled as if to pass off her comment, but she knew better. She also knew better than to press it.

"The case ended okay for you and the firm?"

"And for us," he said. "No one touched your place. It was a worry, and I'm glad we took the precaution of getting you out of town."

She nodded. "Are you going back to the office after we get home?"

"Yeah," he said. "I've got a couple of things to do."

It was the usual miserable slog up the 405 to Sunset where he got off in order to get to Hollywood. Yeah, Hollywood, he snickered to himself, the fabled cinematic land of enchantment where thousands of talented young people flocked only to end up working crappy low-wage jobs waiting hopelessly for the big break that would catapult them to stardom on the big screen; a dream that would never be fulfilled.

He dropped Abby off at the apartment and helped her in with her stuff. Then he went and got the mail for both of them which had accumulated to pretty hefty stacks. After she was settled, he gave her another kiss before he left.

"I missed you," he said.

"Me too."

"Dinner?"

"Sure," she agreed.

He gave her another kiss and with that walked out the door. As she watched him go, she touched her lips thoughtfully. Something had changed.

Instead of going to the office, Taylor headed in the opposite direction. It didn't take him long before he was pulling into the familiar parking lot. There were just a few cars there, and he pulled into his usual spot. He got out of his ride and entered his accustomed refuge from the trials and tribulations of the world. Yusef Lateef's "Love Theme from Spartacus" was playing over the sound system as he walked in.

"Ah, the prodigal son returns," called out Barney from behind his counter. "'Bout time!"

Taylor smiled tiredly. "Gotta latte for a thirsty man?"

Barney chuckled. "Well, it's clear that even a trip round the world hasn't changed you."

"Hey, lemme tell ya, I had lattes every day whenever I wanted them. These cruises. You otta see the food. It just keeps coming and coming."

"And the lattes?" asked Barney.

"Good, but nowhere as good as yours."

Barney chuckled and worked on Taylor's brew.

"And do I have one crazy yarn to tell you. I also brought you a couple of presents," said Taylor.

"Presents, bah! I was worried about you."

"You don't know the half of it. We were up against some really nasty hombres: Murder Inc. And not only that, but..."

Suddenly, Taylor's phone rang.

"Gimme a second, Barn," he said as he checked the number. "Huh, no one I know," he added as he punched the button. "Hello," he answered.

"Mr. Taylor."

"Yeah. And you are?"

"My name's Fenton Kavanaugh."

Taylor thought for a second. Then his eyes narrowed. "Fenton Kavanaugh... *The* Fenton Kavanaugh. Yeah, I know who you are," replied Taylor with a deprecating tone in his voice. "So, whaddaya want?"

"You caused me the loss of something I went to a great deal of trouble to get."

"And some cash too, as I recall," he added saucily.

"That too."

"Well, sorry sir, but that's what happens when you consort with scum who go around murdering nice people."

"Little people aren't my concern. With my wealth and position, I can get whatever I want accomplished. Anything."

"That a threat?"

Kavanaugh chuckled. "I don't threaten, Mr. Taylor. All I can say is that what you did affected me negatively, and I never put up with that kind of treatment without exacting retribution."

Taylor snorted a laugh. "Retribution's a two-way street, my friend," he said. "You ought to think about it to save yourself more trouble than you've already got. If you don't believe me, go ask Mike Matsen what he thinks about retribution now."

"I'm not impressed."

Taylor shook his head. "I don't care. Guys like you just never get it. Yeah, I've heard about you. A multi-billionaire who uses his wealth to destroy what is good about our people, our nation just because you can."

"Really, Mr. Taylor, you do go on."

"Well, Mr. Kavanaugh, let's be clear before you start indulging in the same kind of stupid thinking that lost you your car, your money, and ended with the death of five people. I keep running across the same arrogant morons like you who think a big bank account or a top government position is their license to victimize the world and everyone in it. You actually believe you can escape responsibility for the evil deeds you commit without ever paying for them."

"There is no good or evil. There is only the application of power."

"You just go on believing that. Because for me, you're just another arrogant slimeball who'll eventually get what he deserves. I've seen it happen before; I'm sure it'll happen again."

With that, Taylor rang off and tossed his phone on the counter.

"Was that was for real?" asked Barney.

"Yeah. But what I told him still goes."

"Huh... I suppose there'll always people who stupidly believe they can win against the house," said Barney as he dried a glass.

"That's all right as long as there are always guys around like us who'll call them to account. Which reminds me. Do you remember the time we met Beatrice Jolly?"

"Malcolm's pal? The UFO lady and her friends?"

"Yeah. Well the last couple of days on the trip I had a lot of free time on my hands. I got in contact with her because I'd met one of her old friends, a Professor Ulrich Kaiser who told me one wildass story."

"What about it?"

"Did you ever hear what supposedly happened to Admiral Byrd in 1947 when he took a flotilla of ships on an expedition to Antarctica and supposedly encountered a lost civilization underground at the South Pole..."

THE END

9 798848 100648